**Olivia woke from yet another dream
of wind-blown fire.**

Stubbornly, she kept her eyes closed, hoping to get back to sleep. She'd already been awakened like this at least half a dozen times. Enough was enough!

But this time, the smell of smoke hadn't vanished with the dream. And she could still feel warm gusts of wind on her face...

Olivia sat up abruptly, shoving her well-worn blanket aside. Lurching to her feet, she looked around, trying to orient herself.

Finally, she spotted the path that led toward Mollusk Town. At almost the same moment, a flicker of light appeared through the trees to the left of the path, from the direction of the Trilobur patch—

Flames! she realized with a gasp.

This time it wasn't a dream—the fire was real!

VISIT THE EXCITING WORLD OF

IN THESE BOOKS:

Windchaser by Scott Ciencin

River Quest by John Vornholt

Hatchling by Midori Snyder

Lost City by Scott Ciencin

Sabertooth Mountain by John Vornholt

Thunder Falls by Scott Ciencin

Firestorm by Gene DeWeese

The Maze by Peter David

Rescue Party by Mark A. Garland

Sky Dance by Scott Ciencin

Chomper by Donald F. Glut

AND COMING SOON:

Survive! by Brad Strickland

DINOTOPIA
FIRESTORM

by Gene DeWeese

Random House 🏠 New York

For Esther Ansfield,
not a Commander this time
but still an expert in her field
—G.D.

The publisher's special thanks to James Gurney
and Dan Gurney and Scott Usher

www.randomhouse.com/kids
www.dinotopia.com

Library of Congress Catalog Card Number: 97-66111
ISBN: 0-679-88619-2
RL: 5.7

Printed in the United States of America   June 1997
10 9 8

Cover illustration by Michael Welply

FIRESTORM

Windy Point

Crystal Caverns •

The Hatchery •

Baz •••

Pooktook •

Volcaneum •

Palango River

Hadro Swamp

Waterfall City •

GREAT CANAL

Sculpted Cliffs •••

•• The Time Towers

Cornucopia •

Treetown •

Deep Lake

• Bent Root

Temple Ruins ••

NORTHERN PLAINS

CRACKSHELL POINT

BACKBONE MOUNTAINS

Rocky Pass

Prosperine •

Sapphire Bay

• Poseidos
(sunken)

Amu River

RAINY
BASIN

SKY GALLEY CAVES •

Tentpole of the Sky •

Sky City •

Thermala •

Sauropolis •

Dolphin Bay

Canyon City •

Ancient Gorge

Red Rapid Canyon

The Portal

FORBIDDEN MOUNTAINS

Pteros •

Warmwater Bay

Culebra •

The Sentinels

GREAT DESERT

OUTER ISLAND

BLACKWOOD
FLATS

• Chandara

Dragonfly Coast

Cape Turtletail

CHAPTER 1

So *this* was the fabled Round Table Hall!

It was the most wonderful thing Olivia had seen in all her twelve years. It was even more magnificent than she had imagined. The table itself, larger than most people's houses, glittered like gold. Windows that stretched to the ceiling looked out on the mist-filled wonder of Cloudbottom Gorge.

And gathered around the table were all the Habitat Partners, human and saurian alike. Even Lightwing, the Skybax half of the Aerial Partners, was there, despite his species' well-known dislike of enclosed spaces.

And they were all waiting.

Waiting to hear about the new plant that *she* had discovered!

Olivia looked down and saw that she held the plant in her hand.

Proudly, she lifted it up for all to see.

A hush fell over the gathering. Even Hightop, her Plateosaurus partner, looked down at her in silent approval. There was no doubt left in her mind. After this discovery, she would be made an apprentice to the Forest Partners!

"Please," Bracken, the human half of the Forest Partners, urged her, "tell us about this marvelous plant you have discovered."

Olivia nodded eagerly, but before she could speak, she heard the huge doors behind her opening.

Suddenly, someone was standing beside her. It was Albert, a boy from her village a couple years older than her. But what was he doing *here?*

"Tell the Partners where you found it," he demanded sternly.

Olivia opened her mouth to speak, but no words came out. Suddenly, she couldn't remember where she'd found the plant!

And the plant itself was withering and turning to dust in her hands!

Looking up, she saw that the Partners were no longer smiling at her. They were frowning. Bracken was looking at her and shaking her head with disappointment.

Slowly, Albert unrolled a scroll, holding it up for the Partners to see.

"Here is what she *should* have brought you. A map showing where the plant can be found."

Her face flaming, Olivia lowered her eyes in shame. How could she have forgotten! Albert had told her a million times to take careful notes, to draw sketches and make maps. But she'd seen the plant and known instantly that it was important…

Olivia lifted her head and tried to apologize. "Next time, I promise. Next time—".

But suddenly, she was being drowned in a sea of scrolls. They were showering down out of the sky, piling up on the floor around her, suffocating her. Scrolls full of notes, drawings, maps, diagrams, everything she'd forgotten in her haste.

"Here is the information you need," Albert said.

"But I found it!" Olivia tried to shout, but no words came out. Her tongue felt huge and bloated. The only sound she could make was a rumbling growl. No matter how hard she tried—

Suddenly, Round Table Hall was gone, and Olivia found herself in total darkness. The rumbling growl from her dream—her nightmare!—still echoed in her ears. For one panicky moment, she couldn't think of where she was.

But then the damp, chilly ground she was lying on reminded her. She and Hightop were in the jungle.

She wasn't making any discoveries. She was making a list, an extremely long list. Or she would be, as soon as the sun came up. Then she would once again start identifying and writing down every single species of plant she found, no matter how ordinary.

She and a dozen others scattered about the area, including Albert, had been at it for a week and would likely be at it for another four or five. Like the others, she carried a number of scrollbooks for taking notes.

Each was a collection of short scrolls, carefully flattened and laced together along one edge. She had already almost filled her first.

Albert had worked with Bracken before and had been trying to help Olivia become an apprentice. When Albert had told her he'd talked Bracken into including her on the team, she'd been ecstatic. She loved the outdoors, particularly the forests, even if it did mean sleeping on the ground or getting caught in bad weather now and then. Approaching rain had a smell that was even better than fresh-baked bread. And sunlight, as it sparkled down through a canopy of leaves after a storm, could make her forget the discomfort of wet clothes.

Very few twelve-year-olds, she knew, were chosen for the spot-check surveys the Forest Partners conducted. They were an important part of making sure the forests and jungles stayed healthy. If new types of plants had appeared or old plants disappeared from an area, the Partners would have to find out why. Usually such shifts were just a normal part of the ever-changing nature of the land. But every so often, changes meant that something was wrong. At times like that, the Partners and scientists got together and decided what needed to be done.

And this time, Olivia was right in the middle of it. If she did well—if she didn't mess things up the way she had in her dream—she really *might* be made an apprentice.

The only trouble was, she hadn't realized how many different plants there were. It would take *forever* to write down the hundreds of names and descriptions and the thousands of locations. She grimaced in the near-darkness. She had always had trouble concentrating on tasks like that, where you did the same thing over and over for hours on end.

Just then a sound, part rumbling growl, part hissing scream, came from somewhere in the night, knocking all thoughts of the survey from her head. It sounded just like what had come out of her mouth in her dream.

It was what had awakened her! Something was out there in the darkness!

But the darkness wasn't quite as deep as it had been moments before. The moon was edging out from behind the clouds, and she could actually see the shadowy shapes of trees and ferns all around her.

For a moment, she thought about heading for the nearest Refuge, but only for a moment. For one thing, she wasn't sure she could find one of the hillside caves, even if it were daylight. For another, running around trying to find it would most likely attract the very things the Refuges were supposed to protect you from—meat-eaters that had wandered over from the Rainy Basin, just a few miles away.

"Hightop!" she called, her whispered voice a loud hiss. "Did you hear that?"

The big Plateosaurus, who never slept very

soundly, reared up on his massive hind legs with a start. His long neck whipped his head at least fifteen feet in the air as he looked around. After a few moments, he lowered his head and looked down at Olivia from a height of only eight or nine feet.

"I could hardly avoid it with you practically shouting in my ear," he said. The actual sounds he made were a series of muffled honks and rumbles, but Olivia understood them almost as well as the Plateosaurus understood her speech.

"Not me, silly! It was out there somewhere," she said, waving her hand in the general direction of the noise. "It sounded like something was growling. Something big!"

Hightop's head swayed from side to side on his long neck, a sure sign he was not particularly happy with her. "My dear young lady," he said—or so Olivia chose to translate his carefully enunciated honks and rumbles. "We are in the jungle, just a few miles from the Polongo River and the Rainy Basin. A certain amount of rowdy behavior should not come as a complete surprise."

"But aren't you curious? Don't you want to know what it is?"

"Not particularly. Whatever it is, it can do quite well without being identified by either of us. Now I suggest you go back to sleep and allow me to do the same."

"But what if it's dangerous?" A tingle ran up

Olivia's spine at the thought. She didn't really want it to be dangerous, of course, and since they weren't actually *in* the Rainy Basin, it probably wasn't. Still, it was exciting to think about.

And meat-eaters *did* come across the Polongo now and then. It had been easier than ever the last few weeks. The so-called Rainy Basin hadn't been living up to its name, and the river was creeping lower every day.

"Suppose it *is* dangerous," the Plateosaurus grumbled. "Unless I'm missing something, I'd say that's all the more reason not to attract its attention. I don't look forward to becoming a meal for some creature with more teeth than brains. I can only assume you don't, either. Although," he added, bringing his bluntly rounded nose down to within a few inches of her face, "there are times when you make me wonder."

Olivia sighed but couldn't help smiling at the saurian's mock sternness. He was right, of course.

Besides, the noise had probably just been Thunderfoot. Albert and his Chasmosaurus partner were camped no more than three or four hundred yards away, and Thunderfoot *did* have bad dreams now and then. Bad noisy dreams, or so Albert had told her when they'd started out on this survey.

She grinned, thinking how it must have sounded to Albert. He would've been only a few feet from the source instead of a few hundred yards.

"You're right," she said, getting rid of the grin before the Plateosaurus could notice and comment on it. "Good night."

Lying back down as Hightop watched sternly, she was sound asleep in only a minute or two.

Four hundred yards away, Albert was trying to go back to sleep as well. It was taking him a little longer, however. At least his ears weren't ringing, thanks to the new sleeping arrangements. On this mission, Thunderfoot was spending his nights several hundred feet from where the boy slept.

The apologetic Chasmosaurus had suggested it himself, and Albert hadn't argued. Thunderfoot didn't have noisy dreams every night, but when he did, it was a real fossil-maker for anyone sleeping nearby. Sort of like being woken up by lightning hitting the tree you were sleeping under, Albert had told Olivia once.

It would be bad enough even from Olivia's distance, he thought. It would certainly have been enough to wake her. He couldn't keep from grinning for just a moment. This would be the first time she'd heard it. With her vivid imagination, she'd probably conjured up all sorts of monsters out there in the dark before realizing what it really was.

Then he felt a twinge of guilt and hoped she hadn't been too shaken up. She was, after all, only twelve. Maybe he'd been wrong to urge Bracken to include her in the group.

Albert shook his head silently in the darkness. He'd had this same argument with himself a half-dozen times before. She was too young, too reckless, to ever become an apprentice, one part of him said. But she also had the quickest mind of anyone from their village. In her haste, she could overlook things that were right in front of her, but at the same time she could spot patterns that no one else noticed. Which was just the sort of ability that could prove helpful in almost any mission for the Forest Partners.

To watch over the health of the forests and jungles, you needed to look not only at hundreds of individual plants. You needed also to be able to see them all at once, to see the patterns of the forests.

He was still arguing with himself when he drifted back to sleep.

CHAPTER 2

Olivia blinked in disbelief as she peered down into a jungle ravine early the next afternoon.

"A Trilobur!" she almost shouted.

"I beg your pardon?" Hightop turned from his perpetual lunch, munching at leaves ten and fifteen feet above the ground. He eyed the girl suspiciously. "*Arctium longevus* doesn't grow in the jungle," he said.

"I know it doesn't! But there it is." She pointed at a narrow ledge sticking out from the side of the ravine about a third of the way down. The cluster of thistly purple flowers poking up through the tangle of other vegetation was unmistakable. "See?"

The big Plateosaurus lowered his handlike front feet to the ground and moved cautiously toward the ravine. The purple streaks and splotches on his green and brown hide almost glittered as he passed through a patch of sunlight. Then he was at the edge of the ravine, looking down to where Olivia was pointing.

"It does *look* like a Trilobur," he said after a moment.

"That's because it *is* one."

But even as she spoke, Olivia felt a twinge of doubt in her stomach. This wasn't the sort of thing she could take for granted. If it really was a Trilobur, the discovery went way beyond the sort of thing that was usually found in a spot check. It could make her famous, as in her dream!

At the very least, it would make Bracken take her seriously as a possible apprentice.

After all, the Trilobur—or *Arctium longevus,* as the elders and scholars insisted on calling it—was arguably the single most important plant in all of Dinotopia. Its leaves were used to make healing medicines for both humans and saurians.

And its roots were used to make Trilobite Tea— *the elixir of life,* some called it. Every Dinotopian began drinking it at the age of twenty-four. Every Dinotopian, that is, who wished to live to be "as old as a Trilobite." For the tea healed not just illness but age itself, at least for a century or two.

But it wasn't supposed to grow even this far into the jungle. It was found most often in the plains, fairly often in forest clearings, but never in the jungle. And people had been looking long and hard, ever since its remarkable properties had been discovered thousands of years ago.

Not that the plant was in short supply. Most villages outside the Rainy Basin had their own small patch. And everyone, no matter where they lived, had

11

an ample supply of the dried leaves and roots.

No, the worry was that it might someday be in short supply. There were tales of long-ago times when a mysterious blight had threatened to wipe out the plant, a blight that had been defeated only by fire. The tales, however, were just that. Tales. No one now alive remembered the blight firsthand, and few Dinotopians believed the blight was anything but a tale. A fairy tale, some said.

Even so, many worried that the blight, if real, might someday return. And if it did return, the more widespread the plant was, the better. The more places it grew, the more likely it would be to survive.

"I'll make sure it's a Trilobur," Olivia said. "I'll go down and take a closer look."

Hightop backed away from the ravine and looked down at her. "I thought you said you were afraid you might not be able to get back out once you went in."

"I'm not going down to the bottom, just to that ledge. It's not so far down. If I get stuck, you can lower your tail over the edge and pull me up."

Hightop arched his neck, an indication of disapproval—or concern—that Olivia was very familiar with. "Perhaps we should call one of others to help," he said. "I understand Albert is quite good at scrambling up and down in such places."

"No! I don't need any help!" She wasn't about to go crying to Albert the first time she ran into a problem. The last thing she wanted to do was make him sorry he'd talked Bracken into including her on this survey.

Besides, this was *her* discovery, not his.

Hightop's neck arched even more, but instead of objecting further, he said, "As you wish. But don't say you weren't warned." He returned to his munching of leaves, but stayed close to the ravine.

Carefully tucking her scrollbook into her backpack, Olivia looked down the bank toward the plant and the ledge it perched on—and suddenly remembered why she hadn't gone down before.

For one thing, the sides of the ravine were very steep. For another, she knew that several of the vines along the ravine wall had nasty thorns hidden beneath their innocent-looking leaves. For yet another, *something* in the ravine had been irritating her eyes. They'd been watering and itching on and off all morning. As she looked over the edge, they started watering again.

But now she didn't have a choice.

She took a last look at Hightop. The Plateosaurus was pointedly ignoring her. Cautiously, Olivia eased herself over the edge.

And started down.

Her feet were hidden by the thick vegetation, so she had to feel for each new toehold. With her hands, she did her best to avoid the vines, but she wasn't entirely successful. Thorns were everywhere, snagging at her sleeves and scratching the backs of her hands.

Halfway down to the ledge, her watering eyes be-

13

gan to itch. Even if she'd had a free hand, Olivia knew she didn't dare wipe them. She'd tried that the first time it had happened, earlier that.morning, and it'd only made them worse. The only thing that helped was washing them with water from her canteen. Which she couldn't get to at as long as she had to hang on with both hands to keep from falling.

Worrying less about the thorns than her eyes, Olivia scrambled down the ravine wall until, finally, she was able to twist about and jump the last couple of feet to the ledge. As she landed, one foot twisted beneath her—the ground, hidden by the vegetation, was more uneven than she'd thought. She was able to keep her balance, but just barely.

Fighting down a growing urge to scrape at her eyes, Olivia wet a spot on her sleeve with the water from her canteen and used that to wipe the tears and sweat from around her eyes. She sighed in relief as the itching faded to a bearable level.

Cautiously, she took a couple of steps toward the thistly purple flowers growing near the outer edge of the ledge. Hunkering down next to them, she pulled her scrollbook from her backpack.

As she leaned close, her heart sank. The plant *wasn't* a Trilobur! It was barely two feet tall, much too short for a full-grown Trilobur. And the leaves, which she hadn't looked closely at from above, were the wrong shape.

But whatever it was, it was definitely something

she didn't recognize, something unusual for this area. Which meant she would have to make a detailed sketch of it.

If she could get her eyes to stop watering and itching long enough, that is. If it got any worse, she wouldn't be able to see well enough to sketch *anything*.

Worse, the itch seemed to be spreading to her nose, where it was trying escape through a sneeze. For a moment she struggled to keep it in, but then, still hunkered down, she lost the battle and was shaken by a sneeze so explosive it almost knocked her off balance.

A second sneeze followed, more violent than the first. Olivia felt herself rocking backward on her heels, unable to stop. Instinctively, she dropped her scrollbook and thrust her hands out behind her. But her hands struck the ground at the very brink of the ledge. A small section of the ground gave way beneath her weight.

Before she knew what was happening, Olivia was falling through the air, then crashing into the thicket below the ledge and sliding and tumbling down the ravine wall!

CHAPTER 3

Finally, Olivia came to a bone-jarring stop, flat on her back in a tangle of weeds and vines. The world spun dizzily around her.

She dug her fingers into the soft ground in an attempt to anchor herself, but her grip was shaken loose a moment later by another sneeze. At least the sneeze seemed to stop the spinning and the dizziness, but her eyes were itching even more and—

"Olivia? Are you all right?"

Blinking to clear her eyes, she looked up and saw Hightop peering down at her, his huge head lowered a foot or two into the ravine. A half-chewed leaf fluttered down toward the ledge she'd just fallen from.

"Good question," she muttered between sneezes, struggling to sit up. Her hands were scratched, and there were half a dozen tears in her loose-fitting green-and-yellow blouse and breeches.

But nothing hurt *too* badly, she decided. And she could move everything. In fact, when she sneezed, everything—all of her body, from head to toes—*did* move.

"Olivia?" the Plateosaurus honked more loudly, lowering his head even further into the ravine.

"I'm all right!" she yelled up at him. "I—*achoo!*—think."

For another moment, Hightop peered down at her, making sure she really *was* all right. Then, with a snorting sound she'd long ago decided was a Plateosaurus version of a chuckle, he straightened up and regarded her from his usual regal height. This time it was made even more impressive by the thirty- or forty-foot depth of the ravine.

Olivia sneezed. "All right!" she yelled up at him before yet another sneeze overtook her. "Get it over with. Say 'I told you so,' then get me out of here before my head completely explodes."

"I did warn you, you know," he said, turning away. "I'll fetch Albert," he went on, his honks and rumbles fading, "as I should have done before."

"No! Wait!" she yelled, but there was no response. Olivia could hear the receding thud of his feet and the crunch and crackle of the underbrush as he picked his way through it.

Terrific! she thought, the sting from her scratches driven from her mind. *Just terrific!*

Albert would never let her live this down. It would be the tree house all over again. Six years ago, she'd managed to climb up into a tree house, but she'd frozen and hadn't been able to get back down until Albert had come back. He'd just stood under the tree and laughed. Finally, he'd told her about the rope ladder. It had been rolled up in the corner, only three or four feet from her, the whole time.

But this was worse. She wasn't six anymore. She was twelve, almost thirteen, and hoping someday to become an apprentice to the Forest Partners. Albert knew how much she loved the forest and had been trying to help her. He'd gone out on a limb to get her on this mission, and now she was messing it up. For both of them!

With desperate, itchy eyes, she searched the ravine. There had to be *something* she could do!

Albert looked up from his scrollbook. Something was coming toward them, something big and in a hurry.

For a moment he wondered uneasily if it could be a meat-eater from the Rainy Basin that had wandered across the Polongo.

But Thunderfoot, he saw at a glance, wasn't reacting. The Chasmosaurus was doing what he did most of the time—selecting his next mouthful of food.

A moment later, Albert saw why Thunderfoot wasn't worried. It wasn't a meat-eater approaching, it was Hightop. His purple-streaked head had just popped out of a wall of vines a hundred yards away and was swiveling around on his long neck, searching.

Albert called out to the Plateosaurus.

"Albert!" Hightop honked loudly the moment he'd spotted the boy. "Olivia could use your assistance."

Stabbing a small pennant into the ground to mark his place, Albert headed toward Hightop at a run. "What happened?"

The Plateosaurus explained as he hurried back the way he had come. Thunderfoot followed close behind.

"It was right there," Hightop said, coming to a stop at the very edge of the ravine.

Albert lurched to a stop and peered down. "Are you sure? I don't see her."

"Of course I'm sure!" Hightop honked. "There— you can see where she lay."

"I can see where *something* lay." Albert was starting to really worry. It was a long way down. "Why didn't you stop her?"

"You've known her longer than I have. Have *you* ever tried to stop her from doing something she wants to do?"

Albert sighed. The saurian was right. Besides, it didn't matter whose fault it was—

Behind them, Thunderfoot gave a soft bellow. "There's something back here you should see."

Albert spun around. The Chasmosaurus wasn't very talkative, but when he *did* speak, Albert had learned to listen.

Olivia was emerging from a thicket several yards farther along the edge of the ravine. "I *told* you I didn't need any help," she said as the three of them just stared at her.

"I believe your exact words were, 'Get me out of here,'" the Plateosaurus honked. "In any event, you look terrible, even for one of your species."

"As if you could tell from way up there!"

"He's right, Olivia," Albert said sternly, cutting off their friendly sniping. "You really have to get those cuts cleaned up. It would be best if you—"

"They're just scratches, not cuts!" Olivia said, quickly opening her canteen and wetting a cloth. She wiped at the blood on one of her arms and winced.

"Here, let me do that," Albert said.

Reluctantly, Olivia gave in as Albert took a clean cloth of his own and carefully began to scrub the dirt and blood away. He was relieved to see that they *were* just scratches, not cuts.

He was dabbing some salve on the worst of them when a leathery fluttering sound filled the air.

Looking up, they saw a pair of Dimorphodons flapping earnestly down toward them. The creatures' three-foot wingspans were just short enough to allow them to descend through the narrow and uneven openings in the canopy of treetops.

Olivia almost forgot the pain of her scratches as she watched the dun-colored pterosaurs with their trailing, diamond-tipped tails and blunt, reddish beaks. In her and Albert's home village of Camaraton, she had seen such messengers occasionally, but never had they stopped and spoken to her. They had always been on their way to someone else, someone important enough to have one of these creatures search them out and deliver their memorized messages.

Albert seemed equally impressed, for he fell silent the moment he saw the little pterosaurs. Even Hightop looked up, though he didn't stop munching on his latest mouthful of leaves.

One of the creatures aimed directly for the Plateosaurus and fluttered to rest on his back. The other headed for Thunderfoot and settled onto the huge bony crest that stuck up like a mottled green, stiffly starched collar at the back of the Chasmosaurus's skull.

"What is it?" Olivia asked loudly. "What message do you bring?"

Her words, however, had no effect. With a faint rustling sound, they neatly folded their wings and looked around. With their wings tucked in, they looked much smaller than they had in flight, little bigger than parrots.

Hightop swiveled his head around until he was staring at the pterosaur on his back from a distance of only two or three feet.

"Well?" Hightop said, bringing his big, blunt nose even closer. "Do you have a message to deliver, or did you just stop to rest on my back?"

Both pterosaurs rustled their wings again. Olivia couldn't help but think of someone fidgeting on a stage before a big speech.

Finally, with one last fluttering fidget, they both began to speak. Luckily, except for Olivia's and Albert's names, the pterosaurs had the same thing to say, and their words were pretty much synchronized.

"The remainder of your survey has been postponed. You and your partner are to go immediately to Round Table Hall in Waterfall City. Your new mission will be explained to you there."

CHAPTER 4

To Olivia, eager to learn why they had been summoned, the trip seemed to take forever, even with Thunderfoot bulldozing their way through the dense undergrowth. The Dimorphodons had nothing more to say, and she couldn't even get Albert to *guess* at the reasons they'd been recalled, no matter how often she asked.

He would just shrug and say, "Have patience. We'll find out soon enough."

She suspected he was just as anxious as she was to learn the truth, but he'd never let on.

And if the waiting itself wasn't enough, her eyes decided to water and itch every few hours. A couple of times they got all red and puffy, and once she broke into a sneezing fit that almost knocked her off Hightop's back. Holding a damp cloth across her mouth and nose helped with the sneezing. But for her eyes, all she could do was urge Hightop to move faster, to get her away from whatever was causing it.

Finally, their destination came into sight. The river

slowed and widened into Sweetwater Lake. Waterfall City lay before them. Hightop, Albert, and the half-dozen others who had joined them along the way stood on the shore, looking wide-eyed across the water at the awesome sight. Rainbowed mists were everywhere, billowing up from the mighty falls that flanked the city on both sides. Beyond the mists two ancient stepped pyramids looked down on the Outer Harbor. Atop the two huge structures, the Celestial Dome and the Shrine of Mystery glinted in the sun.

But Olivia barely saw them. She looked for only two things, neither of which were visible: The building that housed Round Table Hall and the ferry that would take them across the lake to Waterfall City.

The ferry arrived at last, towed by a pair of plesiosaurs with long, slim necks that made Hightop's look stubby by comparison. Olivia was the first aboard the ornately decorated bargelike vessel. While the others, saurian and human alike, climbed on with ponderous slowness, Olivia hurried as far to the front as the hand-carved railing would allow. She could feel the mist on her face like a gentle, welcoming breeze.

The captain, a plump, white-haired man with a neatly trimmed goatee, looked down at her from his raised platform. The golden braid on his blue and green uniform glinted in the morning sun.

"In a hurry, are we, missy?"

"We all are," she said, glancing back at the others. How much longer could they stretch out the simple process of coming on board? The vessel bobbed slightly as Thunderfoot placed a foot on the deck as delicately as he could. "We have an appointment at Round Table Hall," she added.

The man nodded as the ferry bobbed again, this time for the rest of Thunderfoot. "Ah, important business it must be."

"I imagine it is."

His white eyebrows arched. "Then ye don't know what it is ye've been called in for?"

Olivia shook her head impatiently. "I'm afraid not. The Dimorphodons that brought the message to us—"

"Ah, well," he said, with a faint sigh. "I suppose it might be important, even so…"

"I'm sure—" she began, but he had already turned away to watch the rest of the saurians and their partners come aboard.

A flush warmed her face as she heard Albert chuckling quietly behind her.

Olivia gasped as the doors to Round Table Hall swung open. Even Albert's jaw dropped. Sounds of awe and wonder came from the rest of the group as they entered the huge room.

It's almost like my dream! she thought.

The plush red carpet was as thick and soft as the best-kept lawn. Equally plush, equally red drapes were pulled back from windows dozens of feet high. The only thing missing was a view of Cloudbottom Gorge, but she could feel the tremors caused by the huge waterfalls that fed it.

"It really does have a round table," Albert said softly.

Olivia nodded. It wasn't golden, but it was at least as big as it had been in her dream. A polished wooden doughnut thirty feet in diameter, the table stood more than six feet high.

For those saurians who wanted them, there were resting couches, but only one ancient-looking Stegosaur was using one. Hightop and Thunderfoot simply walked up and stood by the edge of the table, their heads easily high enough to see. For the humans, there were long-legged chairs that had to be climbed like four-sided ladders before they could sit in them.

Almost filling the hole in the center of the table was a pedostenograph for transcribing the proceedings. Enit, the Deinonychus who was head librarian and records keeper, was already standing next to the machine. Soon, he would be hopping from pedal to pedal, his feet striking them the way a two-finger typist's fingers hop from key to key. Running through the machine was a long scroll. A half-dozen words in the Dinotopian footprint alphabet were already printed across its top.

Olivia scrambled up the side of the chair next to Hightop and looked around. She had just noticed that there were still some empty spots around the table when a short, wiry, gray-haired woman scurried into the room. Behind her came the Habitat Partners of Forests, Bracken and Fiddlehead. Fiddlehead was a Chasmosaurus even larger than Thunderfoot. A moment later, the human halves of the Savanna and Aerial Partners, Draco and Oolu, strode in.

The presence of this many Partners sent a new tingle of excitement up Olivia's spine.

Bracken hurried to catch up to the older woman and offered to help her up into her chair but was abruptly waved away.

"I'm only a hundred and eighty," the woman said, signaling Enit not to begin transcribing just yet. "I'm quite capable of seating myself."

"As you wish," Bracken said, but remained close until the older woman was safely seated. Only then did she clamber up into her own chair. Draco and Oolu took the two remaining seats.

"This is Esther," Bracken said as soon as everyone was settled in. "She has long made a study of the Trilobur plant, to which we all owe so much. However, she has some disturbing news for us all."

"Quite so," the woman said, her voice slightly gruff but perfectly clear. "You may have heard of the fire south of Sauropolis on Blackwood Flats some weeks ago."

Olivia opened her mouth to say that she had indeed heard of it but that she understood it had been put out within a day or two. But before she could begin, Hightop swayed slightly, giving her a gentle nudge that rocked her chair.

Albert darted a stern look in her direction, and Olivia realized that the Plateosaurus had done her a favor. Round Table Hall was not a place where eager first-timers like herself were encouraged to speak, unless spoken to. Feeling her face grow warm, she pressed her lips together and watched the speaker through downturned eyes.

"What you probably have *not* heard," Esther continued, "is that the fire was purposely set."

Olivia and several others gasped. Even Enit faltered in his frenzied hopping from pedal to pedal on the pedostenograph. Acts of deliberate destruction on any scale were virtually unheard of. Setting fires, which could destroy both land and lives, was unthinkable.

Unless—

Olivia realized with a start what Esther was going to say next.

"The blight!" Olivia gasped.

Suddenly, every eye was focused on her, and not many of them looked friendly.

"I'm sorry," she said, her face flaming now. "It…it just popped out."

Esther was looking at her intently. "Tell me, young lady—Olivia, is it?"

Olivia nodded miserably.

"Tell me, Olivia, what made you think of the blight?"

The girl gulped. Suddenly, she wished she could shrivel up and vanish.

"I—I'm not sure," she managed to say. "It's just that Bracken said you had bad news about Trilobur, and I thought I saw a Trilobur in the jungle a few days ago, and that made me think of how it doesn't grow there, and how people've always been looking for it in new places, and I guess that reminded me of the blight a long time ago and how they used fire to get rid of it, and when you said someone set that fire in Blackwood Flats—well, *no* one would purposely set a fire unless they had a good reason, and I guess…"

Olivia's nervous torrent of words trailed off as she looked around at all the faces, human and saurian, still staring at her. "I guess I couldn't think of any other reason someone would start a fire like that," she added. She lowered her eyes to the table in front of her. "I'm sorry. I won't interrupt again. I promise."

Esther nodded. "Thank you, Olivia." She glanced around the table. "However, the young lady is right. It *is* the blight. It is real, and it has returned."

CHAPTER 5

For a moment there was total silence. Then everyone was talking at once. Everyone except Olivia, who was limp with relief that she hadn't made a complete fool of herself.

Finally, Esther held her hands up for attention. "As far as we can tell," she said, "the blight first appeared about three years ago, in the wild."

"But if you've known for three years—" someone began.

"We haven't," Esther said, shaking her head. "We realized what was happening only a few weeks ago."

"But you just said—"

Esther silenced the speaker with a glance. "Let me explain. First, as I'm sure you know, *all* Trilobur plants die after a year or two. Like many plants, they go to seed and die, and the seeds produce a new generation. That means that there are always hundreds or thousands of dead and dying Trilobur plants. A few more in the wild aren't easy to notice."

She looked around the table to make sure everyone understood.

"The difference," she went on, "is that the blight causes them to die *before* they go to seed. Where the blight strikes, there is no new generation. Worse, the land where the blight strikes is forever poisoned to Trilobur. Other plants will grow there, but Trilobur will not. And the blight spreads to surrounding areas, or so it did in the olden days. Nothing anyone did could stop it—until someone thought of fire. Cleansing by fire."

Esther paused, looking toward Enit and waiting until his hopping ceased.

"The flames apparently not only destroyed the blighted plants," she went on. "They also burned away the poison. Once an area was cleansed by fire, newly planted Trilobur grew as well as it had before the blight."

"So we must find the blighted areas and burn them out," someone said, giving voice to what Olivia was already thinking.

But Esther shook her head. "It is not that simple this time. Those early blights, we are told, each began in a single area and spread out from there, season by season. Once a blighted area was discovered, it was simple to burn it out and keep close watch in all nearby areas. When the first sign of premature wilting appeared in a nearby patch, that patch was set afire."

She paused, looking grimly around the group

while Enit once again caught up. "This time, that will not work. For one thing, the lack of rain in recent weeks has made many areas too dry to safely set fires. It's extremely fortunate that none of the fires already set have gotten out of control. But more importantly, the blight this time is following no pattern that anyone can see. It didn't start at a single point and spread outward from that point. Instead, it appears to be springing up at random wherever it chooses. There are already a dozen areas that we know about, from Blackwood Flats to Windy Point, and I fear there may be many more."

"But why does it act so differently this time?" someone asked.

The wiry, gray-haired woman looked around the table once again.

"That is precisely the question we hope to answer. It is the question we *must* answer if Trilobur is to survive. And all of you will play a vital part in answering it."

Olivia's head was still spinning as she and Albert and the rest emerged into the sunshine outside Round Table Hall. Early the next morning, they and dozens of others would be heading out to different parts of the island, from Windy Point in the north to Sauropolis in the south, wherever Trilobur was known to grow. It would be like the spot check that had just been interrupted. But this time their observations would have to be even more detailed, more complete. As a result, they would work in groups of four, two humans and two saurians in each. If one pair missed something, it was hoped that the other would pick it up.

Once all the information was collected and brought back, Esther, the Partners, and other scientists would analyze it.

Then, if everyone was smart enough—and lucky enough—they would be able to figure out what was causing the blight.

And how to stop it.

The thought that she would have a hand in this effort sent a shiver up Olivia's spine.

At the same time, she couldn't help but worry that she would miss something. She was really glad she'd been paired with Albert. He never missed *anything*.

A waiting guide led their group east to the Rosy Morning Promenade, which ran north along the edge of Cloudbottom Gorge itself. The faint rumble that Olivia had heard inside grew now to a deafening roar as countless tons of water poured over White Curtain Falls into the gorge. Olivia sighed enviously at the thought of those who lived and worked in Waterfall City and could see such magnificent things whenever they wished.

Although, she told herself, it was no more beautiful than a sunrise in the forest or the jungle. It was just a different beauty, a different face of nature. And a noisier one, now that she thought about it.

At the far end of the promenade, the guide turned right onto the Bridge of the Winds, leading them over the smaller but still spectacular Gateway Falls. On the far side was the huge, castlelike Haven of the Muses, where they would all spend the night.

Quite a change, she thought with an appreciative grin, *after all those days sleeping on open ground. Better take advantage of it and get a good night's sleep. It'll be back to roughing it tomorrow.*

That evening she found herself having similar thoughts, but now they were about food rather than sleep. In the Haven's banquet hall, the visitors were served a meal the likes of which she had never imagined, let alone seen. Some of the guests, most notably Albert, picked and chose and ate only a few dishes. Olivia, however, enthusiastically sampled virtually every dish that was offered. Often, despite Albert's repeated warnings, she did more than just sample.

A few hours later, as she tossed and turned in her dormitory bed, she regretted it. An exceedingly full stomach, she found, did not make for easy sleep. And a stomach full of unfamiliar dishes was even worse.

The nearby falls dumping countless tons of water into Cloudbottom Gorge didn't help, either. No matter how beautiful they had looked during the day, they were now a huge noise machine that made sleep almost impossible.

Even when she did manage to fall asleep, the sounds invaded her dreams. More than once she woke from nightmares in which the entire Haven crumbled and was carried over the falls like a rudderless boat.

It was times like this that she envied those who could sleep an entire night without a single dream. Usually her dreams were fun. Each night she had a different adventure. But every so often there were nights like this, when her dreams turned nasty and all she wanted was to sleep undisturbed.

When morning finally arrived, the building still stood. Olivia, however, had permanently lost all desire to live in Waterfall City.

"I'd never get another decent night's sleep my whole life," she grumbled to Albert as they emerged into the morning sunlight and headed back across the Bridge of the Winds.

"Oh, this is nothing," he said with a quiet chuckle. "You should be here when the Polongo is high. The falls are *really* spectacular then."

Olivia made a face. "They're quite noisy enough as they are, thank you very much."

"You'd get used to it," he said with a laugh. "Believe me, I know. I lived here several months a few years ago, and I had no trouble sleeping after the first couple of nights. Besides, not every place is like the Haven. After all, it's practically in the middle of Cloudbottom. Other places aren't nearly as noisy."

She wasn't sure she believed him, but it probably didn't matter. There wasn't much chance she'd ever live here for long.

A few minutes later, they were at Jugglers' Plaza, on the banks of Mosasaur Harbor. Hightop and the other saurians were already there. The Sauropod Dwelling, where they had spent the night, was only a few hundred yards away.

Esther and the Habitat Partners were waiting as well. They began passing out maps and issuing final instructions the moment Olivia and the others arrived.

"Dimorphodons have already been sent out to the villages, spreading word of the situation," Esther said. "The message they carry is, of course, short and uncomplicated, so you will have to explain matters to the villagers in much greater detail. The message instructs the villagers to start a continuous watch on the plants in their area. That way, if anything unusual happens before you arrive, they can tell you about it. And once you have fully explained things to them, they can continue observing after you leave. This will, we hope, give us thousands of pairs of eyes in addition to your own."

Esther paused and motioned toward a man standing next to a large cart a dozen yards away. The man spoke quietly to the Pachycephalosaurus hitched to it and the saurian, drab green and tan except for its pinkish head, pulled the cart over to the group.

When they'd stopped next to Esther, the man reached into the cart and lifted out a basket. Something inside the basket was making fluttering noises.

"Each group will be given one of these," Esther said as a Dimorphodon poked its head over the edge of the basket. "They are not for routine reports. Send them back only if you come across something you feel the Partners and I should be told of *immediately*."

A tingle of excitement swept over Olivia at Esther's words. Dimorphodons were not given out lightly. Which meant...

Which meant Esther and the Partners thought it at least *possible* that someone would find something really important.

Something like the solution to the mystery of the blight?

Olivia shook her head sharply, trying to dislodge such unrealistic thoughts. But no matter how hard she tried, she couldn't completely drive them out. It was too exciting!

Then one of the baskets and its fluttering cargo was being settled cozily behind Thunderfoot's huge crest, and they were ready to go.

The next few days, Olivia thought with a shiver, were going to be very nervous-making.

CHAPTER 6

Together with another group, Olivia and Albert and their saurian companions headed north through the heavily forested Polongo Valley. For the first few miles, they skirted Hadro Swamp. As on the inbound trip, Olivia broke into an eye-watering fit of sneezing every few hours. Whatever was causing it must be *everywhere,* she thought with a shudder. After the second fit, she took to keeping a cloth constantly wet, ready to pop over her face the moment her eyes started itching or watering.

Their traveling companions were Carlton and Indira and a pair of playful Triceratops named Grundle and Hoover. They weren't together for long, however. On the second day, the other group turned to the northwest, toward their assigned area around Volcaneum.

Hightop gave a relieved snort when they were out of earshot. He had not enjoyed the Triceratops' games, particularly when they turned into gentle roughhousing. "Creatures like that have far too many sharp points for my taste," he honked softly.

Olivia and Albert continued north, then northeast toward Chimeerney. The further they went, the more concerned they became about the fires Esther had said were being set all over Dinotopia. Hadro Swamp and the jungle areas closer to the Polongo River were in little danger, but here there was increasing reason for worry. What rain had fallen in recent weeks had been spotty at best. Many villages had had none at all. The land might not all be tinder-dry, but several areas were very close.

Early the next day, they came to Gundagai, the first of the tiny villages in their assigned area. At least half the population came running out to greet them as they approached.

"Are you the ones the Dimorphodon told us would be coming?" three or four villagers tried to ask at once. Obviously the Dimorphodons had done their job well.

"We are," Albert admitted, and they were taken immediately to the village's sizable Trilobur patch.

Like most such patches, it looked more like a small field of weeds than a garden. There were no neat rows or any organization at all. Most likely it had started when the villagers found a single plant or two and then "encouraged" them. Usually this meant clearing the immediate area of other plants and letting nature take its course.

After a few years you had a patch like this one,

and you could begin harvesting the leaves and roots.

"I tend the patch," a young man named Barlow said proudly. "There is no blight here."

And there wasn't.

Even so, Albert and Olivia each filled several sheets in their scrollbooks. Albert drew a precise map showing the names and locations of more than two dozen other types of plants in and around the patch.

Olivia was surprised to find several of the almost-Trilobur plants she'd found in the ravine in the jungle. She'd never seen them anywhere before, but now here they were, in a second spot several miles from the first.

Were they related to the Triloburs, she wondered? They were just beginning to bud, as were the dozen or so real Triloburs. From the look of them, they'd both start pollinating in ten or twelve days. After that, it would be another week or two until it was time to harvest the Trilobur roots.

The next village was Narandra, where a tall blond man named Gunnarson took them proudly to a neatly kept Trilobur patch. It was so neatly kept, in fact, that it held *only* Trilobur. There was nothing else, not even a weed. Albert was barely able to fill two sheets in his scrollbook. And there was certainly no sign of the blight.

And so it went for three days, as they zigzagged back and forth through the forests and meadows, hitting a tiny village here, an isolated patch in a forest clearing there.

Until, early on the fourth day, they came to Collicos.

The narrow trail they were on widened and turned into a rough dirt road. At the same time, the forest opened out into a clearing two or three hundred yards across. In the center lay the dozen small, thatched-roof houses of Collicos. Ten or fifteen miles distant on the left, the towers of Volcaneum were visible on their snowy mountaintop. A cloud of steam drifted up from the crater that shared the mountaintop with the city.

Olivia looked around as they approached the little village. Why wasn't anyone coming out to greet them?

Surely they had felt Thunderfoot's approach, she thought with a grin. After the first village, the normally heavy-footed Chasmosaurus had taken to being even more so—probably a trick he had picked up from Grundle and Hoover. From then on, whenever they drew near a village, he would start stomping his feet as he walked. Just to make sure their arrival was noticed, Olivia assumed, which was all right with her.

Had Esther's Dimorphodons missed this village? she wondered as they drew closer and still no one appeared. After all, Dimorphodons *had* been known to get lost or distracted. And with so many being needed, Esther hadn't had the luxury of sending out only the best-trained and most reliable.

"Where does the map say the patch is?" Olivia asked.

"Back there," Albert said, pointing beyond the village to the far side of the clearing. He didn't have to consult the map. "It's in a separate clearing."

Hightop veered off the road in the direction Albert had pointed. "I see a path through the trees," he honked.

Thunderfoot followed closely. A couple minutes later they emerged into a smaller clearing, this one about fifty yards across.

Olivia's heart jumped as she saw dozens of people at the far side of the clearing, clustered around a Trilobur patch. The entire village had to be there!

Sliding down off Hightop's back, she started to run toward the group. "Is it the blight?" she called out. Olivia was surprised at her own eagerness. But if it *was* the blight, and if it was just starting, maybe she could spot what was causing it!

The villagers turned. A young black-skinned man dressed in the well-worn tunic and loose brown trousers and work boots of a farmer stepped out of the crowd.

"Are you the ones from Waterfall City? A Dimorphodon brought a message—"

"We are," Olivia said. "I'm Olivia, and this is Albert."

"My name is Artemus," the young man said. "But no, there is no blight here. In fact, the plants are in better health than we had expected they would be, considering the dryness."

Olivia blinked and halted as Artemus and the other villagers came toward her and Albert. Her eyes were beginning to water. "But why were you all crowded around the patch?" she asked, fighting back a sneeze. "It's not time for a harvest, is it?"

Artemus grinned as he shook his head. "It's nothing to do with the Trilobur. Professor Culpepper just arrived, and he was—"

Suddenly, Olivia lost the fight with the sneeze. As it exploded out of her, she realized the wet cloth she always kept ready was still in a small pouch on Hightop's saddle.

"Here, take this," Albert said, hurrying up behind her. He handed her a cloth he'd wet from his canteen. He'd seen enough of these attacks in the last few days to recognize the warning signs almost before Olivia herself.

Gratefully, she gave her eyes a quick wipe and held the cloth over her nose and mouth like a mask. For the moment, at least, her vision was clear.

Everyone, she realized, was staring at her. Not that she could blame them. She must be a sight.

"Are you all right?" Artemus asked. "Is there anything we can do to help?"

Olivia shook her head, feeling miserable. "Not unless you can tell me why this keeps happening."

When the young man just looked at her in puzzlement, Albert jumped in and explained. By the time he had finished, the entire group had gathered around them, listening sympathetically.

Artemus nodded. "A plant," he said. "It's definitely a plant that's doing it. But there are remedies you can take. My Aunt Dotrice used to have a similar problem. She overcame it with a broth made from part of the plant itself."

Olivia wiped her eyes. "You really think someone could find a remedy for me?"

"Of course. It's just a matter of finding a chemist or an herbalist to prepare it for you. And finding out which plant it is." He looked around. "If it started just now, perhaps it's something in our Trilobur patch."

Olivia squinted at the patch. Then she frowned. There were at least half a dozen of the almost-Trilobur plants.

"When it first happened, I thought it might be those plants that almost look like Triloburs," she said. "But a few days ago, I was right in the middle of a patch of them, and nothing happened."

"Let's see, then."

Artemus turned and darted back to the Trilobur patch. Quickly, he uprooted one of the almost-Triloburs and started back toward Olivia.

"Is it getting any worse?" he asked as he slowly approached, plant in hand.

"Well…it's not getting any better, that's for sure," she said uncertainly.

But by the time he was only a few feet from her, there was no uncertainty left. Even with the wet cloth over her face, the sneezes were impossible to hold in. And her eyes had gone from itching to burning.

"That *must* be it," she managed to say between sneezes.

"Take it away," Albert said abruptly. At the same time, he handed Olivia a second cloth. "And you'd better stay clear of this patch. I'll make all the notes this time."

Olivia didn't argue. "But what *are* those things?" she asked. "And why haven't I been bothered by them before?"

"They are *Arctium culpepperus,*" an oddly accented voice said from somewhere in the midst of the villagers. "And they haven't bothered you before because they did not exist here until I brought them."

CHAPTER 7

Olivia and Albert looked around sharply. After a moment, a small, gray-haired man in knee breeches and hiking boots emerged from the crowd.

"Barnaby Culpepper, at your service," the man said with a bow. "And I offer my most earnest apologies for any difficulty my plants may have caused you."

"You *brought* them?" Olivia's eyes widened. "You're a dolphinback?" She knew the sea people carried stranded travelers to their shore, but Culpepper was the first one she'd ever actually met.

The man nodded. "I was deposited on your shores almost five years ago," he said. "I am sorry that my plants have caused you trouble. However, you should take comfort from the fact that they will be of great benefit to many of your countrymen."

He turned toward a middle-aged, balding man in a well-worn frock coat. "Isn't that right, Mordecai? Has not *Arctium culpepperus* proven useful to you, as I predicted?"

Mordecai lowered his eyes uncomfortably, as did many others standing near him. "I'm sorry, Mr. Culpepper, but I'm afraid not. You see, as I told you when you planted them here three years ago, no one in my village suffers from the illness they are meant to cure."

Culpepper sighed, the same sort of sound Olivia's mother made when Olivia had done something not quite up to her mother's expectations. "Surely," he said, "you do not still maintain that not a single person here suffers from indigestion?"

The man nodded uncomfortably. "Not a one."

Culpepper frowned as he glanced at the other villagers, but then he forced a smile. "As you wish. You are all far more fortunate than I."

Abruptly, he turned toward Olivia and Albert, as if dismissing the villagers altogether. "Did I understand correctly? Are you one of the teams that has been sent out from Waterfall City to investigate the blight?"

"We are," Albert said.

"Good, good," Culpepper said, beaming. "It is fortunate that we have met. I suspect I will be able to help you in your investigation."

"How so?" Albert asked. "Is the blight something you have knowledge of?"

Culpepper shook his head dismissively. "The fact is, I am a trained botanist. I am familiar with plants and their diseases the world over. And I have been studying the plant life on this island for most of the five years since my unplanned arrival."

He gestured at the bulky backpack he carried. "I have dozens of scrolls filled with observations made during my travels. They will, I daresay, be of great interest to my colleagues when I return to England. As will be the existence of creatures such as these," he added, glancing at Hightop and Thunderfoot.

"'Creatures,' indeed!" Hightop honked indignantly. Culpepper gave no indication he had understood. Thunderfoot, still munching on a mouthful of ferns he had found at the edge of the clearing, ignored them both.

Albert's eyebrows went up. "Hasn't anyone told you it's impossible to leave the island?"

Culpepper snorted. "Virtually everyone has told me precisely that. To them—and to you—I say, 'Nonsense!' All I need is a proper boat!" He gave the villagers a look. "I must say, I do not understand you people. On the one hand, you refuse to accept the possibility that anyone could escape this island in a boat. On the other hand, you readily accept the fanciful notion that the root of a plant will make you immortal."

Except for Olivia and Albert and Hightop, everyone studiously avoided Culpepper's glare.

"No one claims the Trilobur plant makes you immortal," Albert said quietly. "All it does is help people to live longer. A couple hundred years, maybe more."

Culpepper laughed derisively. "I suppose you're going to tell me you and your friend here are a hundred years old."

"Of course not. No one drinks Trilobite Tea until they're fully grown. But I do expect to *be* a hundred someday. Maybe even two hundred. My great-grandfather is almost two hundred already."

Culpepper snorted in disbelief. "If this weed is so remarkable, why haven't other lands learned of its properties? Surely you're not going to tell me this island is the only place in the world where it grows."

"And why not?" Hightop honked. He took a long step forward and brought his snout swooping down to within inches of Culpepper's face. "This is, after all, the only place in the world where *dinosaurs* grow! Or have you decided not to believe in us, either?"

"He says—" Olivia began, but Culpepper cut her off.

"I don't need anyone to translate this creature's simple language," Culpepper snapped as Hightop resumed his normal posture, looking down over his snout at the man. "Believe me, young lady, if I had a choice in the matter, I would *not* believe in his existence. There is little I would like better than to awaken in my home in London and discover that this has all been a terrible nightmare. However, I am a scientist, so I am forced to accept the evidence of my senses. What I will *not* accept is that a boat cannot be built that will take me from this island. It's just a matter of time until I find someone willing to construct one for me."

"Others have said the same," Albert said, and half a dozen villagers nodded. "It's been tried more than once, but no one has ever succeeded. One of the shipbuilders who tried—Captain Arneson, I believe—now lectures at the university in Waterfall City. Speak with him if you still have doubts."

"I do indeed have doubts. And I have no intention of spending the rest of my days in this odd land, no matter how hospitable it may be."

"But don't you see?" Albert persisted. "If it were possible to leave this island, someone already would have. And if someone *had* managed to return to the outside world, wouldn't you yourself have known about it? Surely, anyone escaping here would have spread the word, just as you are planning to do. Did anyone in your world even suspect our existence?"

Culpepper seemed to be taken aback for a moment, but he quickly recovered. "Sailors tell stories about all sorts of strange places unknown to the rest of the world," he said. "No one with any sense believes them. But when *I* return, I will have proof. Additionally, my word will be bolstered by my standing in the scientific community, which I assure you is far from negligible."

"The same scientific community," Hightop honked, his neck arching, "that insists that 'creatures' like me can't possibly exist? From what other dolphin-backs tell me about your mistrustful world, you would lose your standing if you tried to convince them of something they didn't want to believe. You might even lose your freedom."

Culpepper drew himself up. "You obviously do not appreciate the esteem in which I am held by my peers."

Olivia braced herself for an angry burst of honking, but the Plateosaurus only made the snorting sound she assumed was a chuckle. "Doubtless the same esteem in which *you* hold *them*," he said. He once again lowered his purple-green head to peer at Culpepper from only a little above eye level.

"But I believe you offered to help us in our mission," the Plateosaurus honked softly. "Perhaps you should explain."

The man scowled at Hightop for a moment, then turned pointedly away from the Plateosaurus. Putting on a stiff smile, he said to Albert, "There is little to explain. As I said, I am on my way to Waterfall City to offer my services to your leaders. It would be helpful if you could direct me to any areas between here and Waterfall City where the blight has been found."

"We've been on the lookout for that very thing," Albert said. "We haven't seen any as yet. But there are many such blighted spots in the hills south of Waterfall City and in Blackwood Flats south of Sauropolis."

Culpepper frowned. "Most unfortunate," he said. "If there *were* any such areas, I could inspect them on my way to Waterfall City. I could perhaps solve the problem on the spot and be able to present your leaders with a solution when we first meet."

"That's all you'll need to figure it out?" Hightop honked skeptically. "A look at the plants that have already died?"

"To one versed in such matters," Culpepper said, "that is often enough. I make no guarantees, of course."

"Of course not," Hightop said, snorting quietly. Olivia didn't know what to think. On the one hand, the botanist was both unpleasant and pompous. On the other hand, he probably knew a dozen times as much as she did about all kinds of plants. And she herself had hoped that if she could see a Trilobur patch when the blight was just starting, *she* might be able to figure it out.

Her thoughts were interrupted by a hand on her shoulder. Startled, she looked around and saw Albert, his eyes squinting, his nose wrinkling, as he sniffed the air.

"I smell smoke," he announced.

CHAPTER 8

For a moment there was complete silence. Then everyone—except Culpepper—was sniffing. Olivia, her nose still stuffy, couldn't smell much of anything.

"You're right," Artemus said, darting looks in all directions.

A moment later, a boy of ten or eleven burst out of the crowd of villagers and raced to a particularly tall tree at the edge of the clearing. Kicking off his shoes, the boy clambered up without hesitation. Artificial handholds fastened to the trunk let him reach the lowest branches in seconds. Disappearing into the leaves, he reappeared moments later near the top, peering out through a spot where some small limbs and their leaves had been removed.

"There!" he called, pointing across the clearing away from the village. "It must be the old patch!" Then he scampered back down.

"Old patch?" Olivia looked around. "Old patch of what?"

"Of Trilobur," the man in the frock coat said,

frowning worriedly. "Until this new patch was established some years ago, we harvested what we needed from a completely wild patch about half a mile from the village."

"It isn't on our maps," Albert noted.

The man shook his head. "No one has thought of it in years." He looked around the group of villagers. "Has anyone seen Delmont this morning?"

Several shaken heads and a chorus of "No's" answered him.

"Who's Delmont?" Olivia asked.

"My grandson," Mordecai said. "He won't be old enough for Trilobite Tea for another ten years, but he was quite worried when the Dimorphodon brought us its message. He came out here to check this patch three or four times each day. He must have decided to check the old patch, too."

"How do we get to the old patch?" Albert asked.

Artemus was already moving across the clearing toward the opposite edge. "This way," he said.

Olivia hurried after him. Culpepper, Albert, and the rest of the villagers followed. Olivia could hear Culpepper puffing already. The two saurians thumped along at the very back of the group.

As Artemus plunged into the trees and ferns, Olivia found herself not so much on a path as on what had once been a path. She couldn't be sure if it was her imagination or not, but the vegetation seemed to be getting drier the closer they came to the fire.

"What possessed this Delmont person?" she heard Culpepper wheeze. "He may well have destroyed vital evidence!"

"Why are you so concerned?" Albert, not nearly so winded, asked. "I thought you didn't believe Trilobur was of any value."

Culpepper's steps faltered for a second. "It doesn't," he said after a dozen yards of wordless heavy breathing. "But it seems to matter a great deal to all of you. I suppose as a citizen, no matter how brief my stay, I consider it my duty to help in whatever way I can."

Olivia stifled a laugh as she suddenly realized why Culpepper wanted to help. Slowing her pace to match Albert's, she waited while Culpepper, increasingly out of breath, fell further behind.

"He wants his boat," Olivia whispered to Albert.

Albert darted her a puzzled look. "His boat?"

Olivia nodded. "He needs someone to build a boat to get him off the island. I'll bet he figures if he saves us from the blight, he'll be such a hero he'll get all the boats he wants."

Albert nodded thoughtfully as they continued to jog. "I see," he said with a faint grin. "Like your desire to make an important discovery so Bracken will accept you as an apprentice."

"That's not the same thing!" she protested, forgetting to whisper.

Albert's grin broadened for a moment, but then it

was gone. "Of course it isn't," he said solemnly.

A little *too* solemnly, Olivia thought, but she didn't say anything. No matter how much she protested, a part of her realized there was at least a *little* bit of truth to what he'd said.

Not that she was *anything* like Culpepper, she told herself firmly. Becoming an apprentice was a perfectly legitimate goal, unlike his silly obsession with "escaping."

Besides, she really *wanted* to study the forest and discover new things, whether she was ever made apprentice or not. Of course it would be a lot nicer if she *was* made apprentice, but—

Then all thoughts of Culpepper and her someday apprenticeship were pushed from her mind. The odor of smoke began to penetrate even her still badly stuffed nose. Ahead, through the trees, she could suddenly see flames.

Speeding up to a run, Olivia and Albert began to overtake Artemus. Culpepper and the villagers weren't far behind when they emerged into another clearing, this one small and unevenly shaped. In the center was a fire, but it was beginning to die out. A boy of about Albert's age—Delmont?—stood only a few yards from its edge, a bucket in one hand. An area eight or ten feet across had been totally burned, but the fire was not spreading.

Almost immediately, Olivia saw why. Completely around the burned area, the once-dry ground had been soaked with water. The bucket in the boy's hand told her how the water had gotten there. Probably from the little creek she had glimpsed from the path.

The boy barely glanced at the newcomers. Instead, he kept close watch on the waning fire. He seemed poised to act, and Olivia saw that the bucket was full. Also, a water-soaked blanket lay on the ground within easy reach. If a flame leapt across the barrier into the dry grass and the bucket wasn't enough to put it out, the blanket almost certainly would be.

But no flame crossed the barrier. There was, she realized, little wind to carry a spark. Which probably meant the boy had planned well. He had waited for a windless day to set his fire.

One by one, the villagers lurched to a stop, then stood watching as the flames shrank and were replaced by smoke, first billows, then wisps. The boy heaved a sigh of relief and set the bucket on the ground.

"Didn't you hear the Dimorphodon's message?" Culpepper had finally arrived. He was gasping for breath but was still able to shout.

The boy jerked around at the sudden angry words. His own features hardened slightly, but his eyes were downcast. "Of course I did," he said quietly. "But every plant was dead. They had died quite some time ago, from the look of them. And this is less than half a mile from our village's plants." He turned toward his father. "I'm sorry, but I didn't dare let it spread. I didn't think burning one patch would—"

"You didn't think at all!" Culpepper raged, beginning to get his breath back. "You just didn't think at all! If I'd been allowed to inspect these plants, I might have been able to determine why they died! But that is now impossible, thanks to you!"

Culpepper looked around at the others, scowling fiercely. Briefly closing his eyes, he shook his head. "There is obviously no reason for me to stay here now." He looked at Olivia and Albert. "I will be on my way to Waterfall City to offer my services to your superior."

Ducking his head in a sharp nod, he turned and barely avoided slamming into Hightop, who had just arrived behind him. Dodging around the saurian, the botanist stalked away.

Hightop swiveled his serpentine neck to watch Culpepper for a moment, then turned back to Olivia. "If no one will build him a boat," he honked softly, "I don't suppose you could convince him to try swimming?"

Olivia's frown dissolved into a laugh. "Probably not."

And with the laugh, her own anger at Delmont seemed to vanish. Which was, she realized, a good thing.

When she had seen the fire, she had been ready to yell at him, too. She probably would have if Culpepper hadn't beaten her to it. After all, Delmont *had* directly disobeyed the Dimorphodon's instructions. And he *had* destroyed whatever evidence she and Albert might have been able to find. But if there was one thing she did *not* want to do, she told herself firmly, it was to sound like Culpepper.

As the villagers comforted Delmont, Olivia turned to Albert. "We might as well look around anyway," she said.

He nodded, and the two of them started walking around the unburned edge of the clearing, peering intently at the ground.

Abruptly, Albert hunkered down for a closer look at something.

"Look at this," he said.

Squinting, she looked where he was pointing. "Another one of Culpepper's plants?"

"It looks like it," Albert said. "Or what's left of one, anyway."

The plant was barely a foot high and nearly dead. Its burs were almost nonexistent, its leaves drooping listlessly.

Olivia quickly looked around. "I'll bet this is another," she said, pointing to a small plant she'd noticed a few seconds before. It was also dying. It had no burs at all, and its spiked leaves were so shriveled they were practically unrecognizable.

But it *was* one of Culpepper's plants, she was almost positive. And it was dead, just like the Triloburs Delmont had burned!

Olivia turned to Albert. "Could the blight be killing Culpepper's plants as well as the Trilobur?" she said. "Just not as fast?"

Albert frowned for a moment, then nodded. "You might be right. Let's see if we can find more of them."

With the villagers' help, Olivia and Albert found one completely dead, shriveled almost-Trilobur even closer to the burned area. They also found five that were in slightly better shape near the edge of the clearing. And beyond the clearing altogether there was one more, looking almost healthy.

For some reason, however, none of Culpepper's plants were making her eyes water, not even the healthy one.

When they talked to Delmont, he said he *thought* he had seen a couple dead almost-Triloburs in the patch before he'd set the fire. Everything else, he insisted, had been growing normally, the usual weeds and grass and a few flowers.

All of which was interesting, but hardly enough to warrant sending a Dimorphodon message back to Waterfall City. Even so, Olivia filled three sheets in her scrollbook while Albert filled five.

On their next six zigzag stops, they found nothing new. There were no more stricken plants, no more burned patches. The notes for one day looked very much like the notes for the day before and the day after.

In three of the patches, there were a few of

Culpepper's plants. As in the first village, he'd planted them three years ago and had just recently been back to check on them. In one patch, .they appeared to have gone to seed early and were quietly withering, while some of the seeds had already sprouted the beginnings of new plants. In two others, the plants were just beginning to form buds.

To Olivia's relief, her eyes didn't water or itch at any of the three patches. And she didn't sneeze even once.

"It's not the plant itself that bothers you, dearie," a ruddy-faced woman in the sixth village said when Olivia remarked on her good fortune. "It's the pollen. You know what pollen is, don't you?"

Olivia nodded. "Of course. It's what goes from one plant to another, so they can make seeds to grow new plants."

"Right, dearie. Trouble for folks like us, it gets to the other plants by floating through the air, and a lot of it goes right up our noses. Back home in Cornwall, it only happened in the fall, but here you don't have proper seasons, so it can happen whenever the urge strikes. Lucky for me, whatever plants had it in for me back home don't exist out here, so I'm okay. Looks like you still have something to worry about, though." She gestured at the plants and the embryonic buds. "You'll be feeling the effects of these in a few days, I wouldn't be surprised."

They didn't stay long enough for Olivia to be affected, but at their next stop, she found that the woman was right. Her eyes started itching a hundred feet from the patch the villagers were taking her and Albert to see. Forcing herself to go on, she quickly spotted a half-dozen of Culpepper's plants in one corner of a patch otherwise dominated by sturdy-looking Trilobur, themselves just starting to blossom.

But there was no sign of the blight. Both types of plants appeared to be thriving, and they quickly moved on, hoping to reach the next spot on their map before nightfall. It soon became apparent, however, that they wouldn't make it. The road they'd been following became a narrow trail and then vanished altogether, and they found themselves picking their way through an unmarked forest.

Another night sleeping on the ground, Olivia thought as the sun touched the horizon. But at least it would be dry. She just hoped the rain everyone was praying for wouldn't show up until she had a roof over her head again. She liked the outdoors and all that, but she preferred the *dry* outdoors.

She was peering into the growing shadows, looking for a likely place to stop, when a Dimorphodon flapped by overhead. It was coming from the south, the direction of Waterfall City. Probably headed for some village farther on, she decided. But even as the thought came to her, the creature wheeled about and swooped down toward her and Albert. Moments later, it settled onto Hightop's back just behind his saddle. It was so close she could hear its whispery breathing and the rustle of its leathery wings as it carefully folded them.

A shiver went over her as she realized it must be from Esther. And that Esther would not have sent this creature out without a very good reason.

Uneasily, she waited as Hightop and Thunderfoot stopped side by side. Albert, too, sat waiting while the Plateosaurus swiveled his head around to watch the little creature.

It, however, was in no hurry. Like the ones that had fetched her and Albert from the jungle, it went through what still looked to Olivia like an extended throat-clearing routine.

Finally, it was ready to begin.

"More burnings are being reported from all areas," it said, parroting what Esther had told it several hours, perhaps a day, before. "None have gotten seriously out of control yet, but it is likely only a matter of time. You must complete your observations as quickly as possible and return to Round Table Hall. Warn everyone you see in the strongest possible terms: No blighted area is to be burned! This is particularly important in your area, where the dryness could lead to disaster."

When it fell silent, Olivia felt both apprehension and excitement ripple through her. She even imagined she could smell smoke in the distance, but when she turned to look, nothing was there.

CHAPTER 9.

"Fire!"

Olivia sat up so abruptly she bumped her head—on Hightop's snout, she realized an instant later. The Plateosaurus was bent low over her in the dim light of a cloudy dawn.

But the light wasn't all that dim, she suddenly saw. There was a flickering reddish glow over everything. Turning abruptly, she saw a wall of fire bearing down on them through the trees. Branches crackled and sparks flew. She could feel the heat of the flames on her face even at this distance.

"I said, 'Fire!'" Hightop honked again, not quite as loudly, then backed off and raised his head to its normal height. "Now that you're *finally* awake, let's get moving!"

Olivia scrambled to her feet and leaped onto Hightop's back. Albert was already clambering onto Thunderfoot a dozen yards away.

Except, she realized a second later, it wasn't Albert.

It was Culpepper!

Albert was still on the ground, asleep. Or unconscious!

Leaping down off Hightop's back, she raced to the boy's side. "Albert!" she shouted, grabbing his shoulder and shaking him violently.

But no matter how hard she shook him, no matter how loudly she yelled, he wouldn't wake up.

"Here, let me help!"

Spinning around, Olivia saw Esther standing over her. And with her were Oolu and Lightwing, the Aerial Habitat Partners.

Olivia blinked in disbelief. Skybaxes couldn't land in the jungle! There wasn't nearly enough space between the trees for them to fit.

"I will take him." This time it was Oolu who spoke. He leaned down and scooped Albert up in his sturdy arms.

For a moment, Olivia thought Oolu was going to drape Albert across the Skybax saddle, but at the last minute he turned toward Hightop. Thunderfoot had disappeared while Olivia had been trying to rouse Albert, but she could still feel the ground shaking from his footsteps.

Olivia clambered again into Hightop's saddle. Oolu literally tossed Albert's limp body onto the Plateosaurus's back just in front of where she sat.

"This way!" Oolu shouted over the crackling of the flames, now almost upon them. He and Esther climbed onto the Skybax and, impossibly, the creature flapped its wings and soared into the sky through a hole that suddenly appeared in the canopy of trees.

Then, to Olivia's utter amazement, Hightop crouched down on his huge back legs and leaped after the Skybax like a cat after an escaping bird. The canopy opened even wider for them than it had for the Skybax.

And they were soaring above the jungle! When she wasn't looking, Hightop had sprouted wings ten times as wide as the Skybax's. Wings so powerful that the wind they created began driving back the flames! Olivia tightened her hold on Albert's tunic as the newly winged Plateosaurus banked steeply to take another run at the fire.

But, suddenly, she was falling!

She'd lost her hold on the saddle and was plunging earthward, the flame-heated air beating at her face.

All she could think as the treetop inferno rushed up to meet her was now she'd never make apprentice.

"Olivia!"

It was Albert's voice, shouting at her as she fell, but she couldn't see him. He should have been falling with her, but—

Suddenly, her entire body twitched violently, like a puppet jerked by its strings.

And she was awake, lying on the ground where she had gone to sleep. She was bathed in sweat, and her heart was thumping so hard she could feel it in her toes.

Albert was leaning over her, his hands on her shoulders. Only a foot or two above him, Hightop looked down at her.

"That must've been a dandy," Albert said quietly. "I was afraid you were going to hurt yourself, thrashing around and yelling the way you were. Are you okay?"

She pulled in a shaky breath. "I think so," she said, looking around to make sure there really wasn't a fire bearing down on them.

And that Hightop wasn't sprouting wings.

Letting her breath out in a relieved sigh, she lay back down. She'd told Albert about some of her other dreams, but she didn't think she'd tell him about *this* one.

At dawn, they sent the newly arrived Dimorphodon back with what little information they had: The patch of Trilobur they'd seen burned, the fact that the blight seemed to be killing Culpepper's plants as well as Trilobur, and a warning that Culpepper himself would be arriving in Waterfall City.

By midmorning, they'd made quick surveys of two of the wild Trilobur patches and were approaching the next village on their map. While they were still hundreds of yards from the village, they were startled by the sound of singing.

"No blight there, I'd guess," Olivia said with a grin. "Isn't that one of the harvest songs?"

Albert nodded and urged Thunderfoot forward. He remembered even better than Olivia the joy that accompanied each harvest in their home village of Camaraton.

Soon they found themselves being welcomed by a crowd of villagers. All were eager to share their good fortune with the travelers.

Despite the lack of rain, more than a dozen plants had budded almost simultaneously twenty days before. From then on, the villagers had taken turns carrying water more than half a mile from a not-quite-dried-up stream, and the plants had continued their development. They had even started pollinating all within the same day. After that, the villagers could almost see the soil bulge as the unseen roots grew and fattened.

Then, just this morning, the time had come for the harvest.

A magical time.

The roots were at their fattest. If not harvested, they would begin to shrivel within hours. The nutrients the plants had stored in the roots would be drained by the growing burs—the seeds that would become the next generation.

It was those nutrients that gave the plant its value. Harvest the roots a few days early, before all the vital nutrients were stored, and it would be of no more value than those of any other plant. The tea made from them would be just tea, not a potion that added decades to life. Harvest it a few days later, after the nutrients had begun to be drained, and it would be similarly ordinary.

But now, at this moment…

Obviously, the villagers told each other, the blight the Dimorphodon had spoken of was not a threat here. And their days of carrying water from the stream had not been in vain.

They had just finished hanging the roots and leaves and flowers up in drying rooms all over the village when the four travelers arrived.

"Come," a tall Asian-appearing woman in colorful garb said as soon as introductions and explanations had been exchanged. "I am Karawinn. We would be honored if you would join us in the brewing!"

Despite the urgency of Esther's message, it was impossible to refuse, particularly when Karawinn brought out her family's own mortar and pestle from a carefully crafted, tightly sealed wooden case. She insisted Olivia and Albert use them to ceremonially grind some of the already-dried roots from previous harvests.

"It will give good fortune to your quest," the woman said as Olivia reluctantly accepted the utensils and a small portion of the dried roots. "These have been in my family for as many generations as any can remember."

Olivia realized what an honor she and Albert were receiving. The utensils themselves were decorated with a dual crest representing both the Trilobur and Karawinn's own family. Normally they were used only by that family, just as they were used only to grind Trilobur roots and nothing else. In that way the purity of the nutrients was maintained. Whatever the roots contained that had brought generations of long life and health to Karawinn's family would continue to do so.

As soon as Albert had had his turn, he carefully, almost reverentially, returned the utensils to Karawinn. Quickly, he explained the urgency of their mission and why he and Olivia must leave before the brewing.

"Of course," Karawinn said. "It is important to us all that you find the source of this blight. And if it does someday strike here, rest assured that we will make the most complete and meticulous observations possible."

Half the village then escorted them to the Trilobur patch. To Olivia's relief, there were none of Culpepper's plants. The Trilobur appeared to be as healthy as they had been told, and by early afternoon the four of them were on their way.

The next few spots indicated on their map were small, completely wild patches in the forest. They located the first one, about a mile past the shrunken Williwaw Creek, in only a couple of hours.

Or rather, they located its remains.

The patch was nothing but ashes, thoroughly doused and stirred. The grass and weeds surrounding the burned-out area were also still damp. Like Delmont earlier, whoever had done this had at least been careful to keep the fire from spreading. He must have carried the water all the way from Williwaw Creek.

But who had done it? Someone with maps like their own? Someone ignoring Esther's warnings, determined to stop the blight the old-fashioned way—with fire?

Hurriedly, they each filled a sheet in their scrollbooks and moved on to the next patch, barely three miles to the north. This time, a dozen healthy plants greeted them. Following Esther's latest instructions, they spent only a few minutes determining what stage the plants were in and if they were indeed as healthy as they looked. Then they raced on.

The next patch was not far from the village of Mollusk Town. Looking at the map, Olivia couldn't help but wonder why a village this far inland was named for seafood. As they neared the village, however, her curiosity took a back seat to eyes that were suddenly itching and a nose that was beginning to run.

"Culpepper," she said, and sneezed.

"If you want to skip this one," Albert offered, "it's all right. I can check it out alone."

She shook her head and urged Hightop on. "I survived it before," she said.

This time, though, was even worse than the other times. According to the map, the patch was a good

71

fifty yards to the side of the trail. How many of those stupid plants *were* there? she wondered.

But there was only one, she saw as she jumped down from Hightop and entered the clearing. The problem was that it was right in the middle of flooding the air with its pollen.

Olivia wiped her eyes with her wet cloth and quickly looked around before they began itching and watering again. But there was nothing unusual. Dozens of Trilobur, the single Culpepper plant, the usual assortment of other weeds and grasses, all seeming to be suffering only slightly from the dryness.

Several of the Trilobur, she noticed, were within hours of pollinating. Olivia smiled. She wouldn't have noticed that two weeks ago, but she'd been watching and learning. Before this trip, she couldn't tell much more than if the plants were budding or not budding or going to seed. But now, after seeing hundreds of plants in all stages of growth, she'd learned to spot the different stages almost as easily as the villagers who determined the proper time for harvest.

Not that this knowledge was getting them any closer to figuring out what was killing the plants, she thought. Her mood darkened along with the twilight sky as another fit of sneezing seized her.

By this time, a half-dozen villagers, having heard either her sneezing or Thunderfoot's walking, greeted them and offered them beds for the night.

Olivia thanked them but declined. "I need to put

a little more distance between myself and that patch," she said between snuffles. "But you go ahead, Albert. No need for both of us to sleep on the ground. I'll see you in the morning."

He protested, but only briefly. A few minutes later, she and Hightop were settling down at the edge of another clearing a hundred yards past the village.

At least in this kind of weather the ground was dry, she thought as she sat down, her back against a small tree. And tonight there was almost a full moon. It gave her enough light to finish the day's entry in her scrollbook. If it stayed clear, they might be able to start moving before dawn in the morning.

Sighing, Olivia finished her entry, then lay down and drifted off to sleep.

Olivia woke abruptly from yet another dream of wind-blown fire. At least this one hadn't involved Esther and a flying Plateosaurus.

Stubbornly, she kept her eyes closed, hoping to get back to sleep. She'd already been awakened like this at least half a dozen times. Enough was enough!

But this time, she realized with a start, the smell of smoke hadn't vanished with the dream.

Not only that, she could still feel warm gusts of wind on her face.

Her eyes snapped open and she sat up abruptly, shoving her well-worn blanket aside. Lurching to her feet, she looked around, trying to orient herself.

Finally, she spotted the path that led toward Mollusk Town. At almost the same moment, a flicker of light appeared through the trees well to the left of the path, from the direction of the Trilobur patch—

Flames! she realized with a gasp.

This time it wasn't a dream—the fire was real!

CHAPTER 10

"Hightop!" Olivia shouted. "Thunderfoot! *Fire!*"

Stuffing her blanket and canteen into her backpack, she slipped into its harness without even looking. As she turned again toward the flames, Hightop and Thunderfoot burst into the clearing from behind her.

"One of you go wake the villagers!" she shouted over her shoulder as she plunged into the forest toward the distant flames.

Before she'd gone more than a dozen yards, Thunderfoot had crossed the clearing and was racing down the path toward the village, shaking the ground as he thudded along. The Dimorphodon had already launched itself from its basket and flapped up and out of sight. A moment later, Hightop was at Olivia's side, slowing enough for her to clamber aboard.

Wrapping her arms around the Plateosaurus's neck, she hung on for dear life as he crashed through the trees and underbrush. Her eyes quickly began to water as they neared the clearing, and a sneeze almost jarred

75

her grip loose. Another hundred yards and it was so bad that she had to close her eyes and simply hang on.

Then Hightop was lurching to a stop. Eyes still shut against the stinging air, Olivia could feel the heat of nearby flames. Quickly, she found the wet cloth she always kept in the pouch fastened to Hightop's saddle. Tears streaming down her face, she wiped her eyes vigorously, then draped the cloth over her nose and mouth.

She opened her eyes—and gasped.

The entire Trilobur patch was ablaze. Flames were leaping a dozen feet in the air. The fire was several times the size of the one Delmont had set. The way the flames were dancing, it looked as if they were creating their own wind in addition to the one that gusted out of the trees.

A massive Saltosaurus stood on the upwind side, just outside the wetted-down area that was—so far—containing the blaze. More than ten meters long, with four elephantine feet and a neck longer than Hightop's, it dwarfed both Hightop and Thunderfoot. Draped across its brown, speckled back just behind a heavy saddle was what looked like a pair of gigantic, limp saddlebags. They drooped well down its sides, more than halfway to the ground.

So that's how the water was carried to the fires, Olivia thought. From the saddle itself dangled a rope ladder, which would be needed to mount a creature this size.

Standing next to the saurian was a large man, grizzled and soot-smeared, watching the fire intently. But, unlike Delmont, his hands held no container of water, no water-soaked blanket. *Not that such things would do any good against a fire this size if it escapes,* she thought worriedly.

Hightop saw the pair, too, and hurried toward them, skirting the flames at a cautious distance. As they reached the upwind side, Olivia's discomfort faded. With a last swipe at her eyes, she stuffed the wet cloth back in the pouch.

The man seemed oblivious to their approach as he continued to watch the flames intently. A look of satisfaction filled his weathered, flame-lit features.

"What are you *doing?*" Olivia shouted over the intense crackling and whooshing of the flames. "There wasn't any blight here!"

The man jerked about, as if startled. "Where did you—" Then he scowled. "You're one of the ones from Waterfall City!" he said, looking accusingly at Olivia.

"That's right," she said, suddenly angry. "And *you're* one of the ones going around trying to burn everything down!"

"I burn only the blighted patches, as our forefathers did. It is the only way the blight will be stopped, no matter what your Dimorphodons say!"

"This patch *wasn't* blighted!" she shouted. "And even if it was, burning won't work this time! We have to find out what's *causing* the blight. That's the only way we'll ever stop it. That's why Esther—"

"We can't wait, not for her or for anyone! No one's going to find out what's causing the blight! And even if someone did, it would be too late! Trilobur would be gone from our land. I myself have seen a dozen patches destroyed just in the last three weeks!"

"If they were all like this one, *you* destroyed them, not the blight! There *wasn't* any blight here! Albert and I inspected this patch just a few hours ago, and it was perfectly healthy!"

The man scowled at her again. "If none of you 'investigators' are any more observant than that, it's no wonder you haven't learned anything useful!" He gestured sharply at the flames. "At least a dozen of the Trilobur plants were shriveled and dying when Delphinia and I came upon the patch an hour ago."

"Waldemar is telling the truth," the Saltosaurus said, its voice a bass version of Hightop's honks and rumbles. "I, too, saw the dying Trilobur. They were quite unmistakable in the lantern light."

Olivia blinked, looking from Waldemar to Delphinia and back. Few Dinotopians lied, even to protect their own skins, and saurians found it almost impossible. Could she and Albert both have missed a dozen or more blighted, wilting plants, she wondered? Could there be a second patch nearby? A patch where the Trilobur plants they had seen still grew?

Suddenly, over the sounds of the flames, she heard

the distant clamor of agitated voices. Shading her eyes, she saw dozens of villagers hurrying toward them through the forest. In their midst was Thunderfoot, Albert on his back.

Olivia was turning back to Waldemar to question him further when a howling gust of wind seemed to set the entire forest to swaying. The rustling of countless leaves and the creaking of thousands of branches drowned out both the fire and the approaching villagers.

Olivia looked at the burning Trilobur patch—and gasped.

At the very edge of the flames, a whirlwind had appeared! She had seen the little vortexes many times before. They would spring up, seemingly out of nowhere, invisible except for the dust and leaves and other tiny particles they picked up. Then they would dance about, turning and twisting in no pattern she had ever been able to see. Eventually they would die out, quietly dropping their feather-light burden wherever they were when their mysterious energy ran out.

But *here*—

This one was growing, as if fed by the energy of the flames themselves.

Nearly as wide now as the wetted strip, it sparkled as it sucked up still-glowing embers of grass and weeds and Trilobur. And sent those embers flying in all directions.

A half-dozen spots beyond the strip burst into flames.

On the other side of the clearing, a second whirlwind had sprung up and was doing the same as the first. Like fiery raindrops, embers were hitting the ground everywhere!

Olivia threw her backpack to the ground and yanked her blanket out, spilling the rest of the contents out on the grass. Throwing the blanket on the wetted strip of ground, she emptied her canteen on it, then snatched it up and raced to the nearest outbreak and began beating at the flames. Waldemar, looking around frantically, grabbed the sodden saddlebags and dragged them off Delphinia's back. They were too big and heavy to lift in the air, but he was able to drag them onto the burning spots, then jump up and down on them a few times before moving on to the next.

Then the villagers arrived, dashing into the clearing. Each carried something—blanket, broom, water bucket—anything that could beat out or douse a fire. Suddenly, they were all around the clearing, attacking every patch of flame—throwing water, beating them out with whatever they carried. Albert was wielding a large broom, and next to him Thunderfoot stomped at the edges of the flames. Hightop was gingerly doing the same at a smoldering patch nearby.

But even as it looked as if the villagers were winning, new embers flew over Olivia's head, high in the air. And one of the treetops, even drier than the grasses below, burst into flames.

A dozen voices screamed, but there was nothing they could do.

Albert, hearing the screams, looked up. For a moment, his mouth gaped, but then he shouted, "Thunderfoot!"

The Chasmosaurus looked up. An instant later, he abandoned his attempts to stomp out the grass fire and pounded across the clearing and into the forest next to the burning tree. Turning around, he lowered his head and crashed against the trunk, shaking the entire tree.

Again he butted against it, and again.

A moment later, Hightop joined him, not battering at the tree with his head but standing half-erect and gripping it with his large, clawed front feet and leaning into it with all his strength. Just below where Hightop gripped it, Thunderfoot smashed into it again, and yet again.

Then the Saltosaurus was there as well. With a huge effort, it lurched upright on its massive back legs and slammed its front feet against the trunk well above where Hightop was gripping it.

Suddenly, a ripping, cracking sound filled the air, almost drowning out the shouts of the villagers.

The tree toppled forward into the clearing. Flaming leaves flew in all directions as the crown hit the ground. A dozen villagers were around it immediately, knocking the burning leaves to the ground and beating them out.

Thunderfoot seemed dazed for a moment, but then, with a shake of his head and huge crest, he returned to stamping out embers in the grass. A moment later, he was joined by Delphinia.

Finally, shortly after dawn, the fire was out. The Dimorphodon came flapping down from somewhere and settled into the basket still on Thunderfoot's back as if nothing had happened.

At one edge of the clearing the villagers were all collecting around Waldemar and Delphinia. Waldemar's broad shoulders were slumped, his soot-streaked face a picture of misery as he apologized and tried to explain.

But the villagers, rather than shouting at him angrily, were comforting him.

Olivia, soot-stained herself, found Albert at the edge of the crowd. Thunderfoot was holding one front foot up while Albert rubbed some Trilobur salve on a couple of spots on the bottom. It was the foot the Chasmosaurus had used in most of the fire stomping.

"You'll just have to be careful for a little bit," Albert was saying. "But this salve will have it good as new in a day or two."

Experimentally, Thunderfoot lowered his foot and began walking slowly in a circle. He limped slightly as he held the burned foot at an angle and tried to keep from putting his full weight on it, but he still moved faster than either of the humans normally would.

Albert turned to Olivia. "Are *you* all right? You were right in the middle of it when the rest of us got here."

"I'm okay," she said. She glanced at the burned out Trilobur patch. "At least I'm not sneezing anymore. But this *is* the patch we looked at yesterday afternoon, isn't it? The one with several perfectly healthy Trilobur plants in it? Plants just ready to pollinate?"

"It is," Albert said, glancing toward Waldemar. "But *he* said a dozen plants were shriveled and dying. He's positive it was the blight."

Olivia frowned. "I know. But even if you pull a plant up by the roots, it doesn't shrivel up *that* quickly. It wasn't even twelve hours!"

"But these did," Albert said. "Unless Waldemar was mistaken in the dark."

Olivia shook her head. "He had a lantern, and Delphinia saw it, too."

"Then the blight *did* kill them in twelve hours." He sighed, a faint smile lightening his smudged face. "It's too bad Culpepper wasn't here. If he'd seen this patch just before the blight struck, maybe he'd have it all figured out by now."

Olivia grimaced. "Sure he would."

Suddenly, Olivia realized what Albert was saying. They'd seen a patch of Trilobur at virtually the moment the blight had struck! And they'd written down everything about it, down to the last detail.

She started to get out her scrollbook, then thought better of it. Nobody took more detailed observations than Albert.

"Albert, your notes!" Olivia said. "You took all sorts of notes on that patch!"

She waited impatiently as Albert dug out his scrollbook. Surely the solution to the mystery of the blight was right there in his notes.

All they had to do was figure it out...

CHAPTER 11

"But it *has* to be Culpepper's stupid plant!" Olivia said doggedly. "It doesn't make sense any other way!"

The sun was setting on a very long day. Contrary to her hopes, she hadn't found an answer in Albert's notes on the burned patch. It had come, instead, from the Trilobur patches they had looked at that day. All six had two things in common. First, every Trilobur, from month-old growing plants to two-year-old, go-ing-to-seed plants, was in perfect health. Second, every patch was completely free of Culpepper's almost-Trilobur. They hadn't been able to find any within fifty yards of the patches.

Albert shrugged as he bent down to apply more salve to Thunderfoot's still slightly tender front foot. "You can't expect the answer to just jump out at you like that. It doesn't work that way."

"*I* know that!" she snapped. "But if one *does* jump out at you, you can't just ignore it."

"Of course not. But you can't accept it without question, either. Especially when there are lots of things it *doesn't* explain. For instance, we've seen lots of patches where both plants are growing side by side."

"Like the one at Mollusk Town!" she said triumphantly. "Twelve hours later, the Trilobur were dying!"

"Then what about the fact that the blight kills Culpepper's plants, too?"

She shook her head. "I told you, I haven't figured *everything* out! Maybe it's a bug or something that came along with the plants from the outside world. Maybe the plants were sick to begin with. And whatever they're sick with kills Trilobur, too. They *do* look a lot alike."

"Except Culpepper didn't bring any actual plants, only seeds."

"And how do you know that? I don't remember him saying what he brought with him."

"How could a dolphinback bring a live plant with him?"

"*I* don't know! Maybe he was on a raft! We'll ask him when we get back to Waterfall City. Anyway, I'll bet the blight has *something* to do with that plant!"

"I'm not saying it doesn't," Albert said, straightening as Thunderfoot gingerly lowered his salved foot. "I'm just saying it can't be as simple as you want it to be." He glanced at the scrollbooks they had both filled in the last few days. "The complete answer may be in there, but I really don't think we've found it quite yet."

And so it went. Even when the discussion trickled

away into nothing, Olivia kept poking the questions around in her head. Finally, seeing that the moon was bright enough to read by, she borrowed Albert's scrollbook again. She fell asleep going through his descriptions and diagrams of the Mollusk Town patch for the third or fourth time.

Even then, her mind continued to worry at the problem, at least if her dreams were any indication. Instead of fire, they were filled with Trilobur and Culpepper's almost-Trilobur.

But they weren't all that much of an improvement. In her dreams, she was constantly flitting from one patch of Trilobur to another. And every single time, she arrived sneezing and scraping at her eyes, just as the plants shriveled and died.

Sometimes it was Culpepper's plant, sometimes Trilobur, and sometimes she couldn't tell one from the other. All she knew was that as soon as she came near they were going to shrivel up and die, and she was going to start sneezing.

But in the dreams, unlike in real life, she could plainly see what it was that was doing it to her. From dozens of yards away, she could see huge clouds of dust hovering around the dying plants. The dust was really pollen, she was sure. She knew, of course, that in the real world, pollen was invisible, but this didn't make her sneezing fits any less violent.

After the first two or three times, she started trying to get away. Each time she saw the clouds, she turned and ran, but they always took off after her like ghostly, demented Skybaxes. As the clouds caught and swarmed around her, her head exploded with sneezes. And while she was sneezing helplessly, the voice of the woman from Cornwall would practically shout at her, "It's not the plant itself that bothers you, dearie."

That was invariably when she would wake up, the woman's words echoing in her mind.

As she had a dozen times during the past few nights, Olivia wished she could shut the dreams off. But that wasn't how it worked. She'd dreamed virtually every night of her life for as long as she could remember, and the few times she'd tried to shut the dreams off, she hadn't had any luck at all.

Nor had she ever been able to consciously decide what to dream about. Whatever came up, came up, and that was that. Usually it was at least interesting. But sometimes, for instance with the fires the last few nights, and now these stupid plants...

Olivia groaned the next time she sneezed herself awake. The sky was brightening in the east. It was dawn already, and she felt as if she hadn't slept at all, as if she'd spent the whole night sneezing, being bombarded by pollen from either Culpepper's plants or the Trilobur itself.

She shook her head. Talk about crazy dreams. Trilobur pollen making her sneeze, making her eyes water. Even when it *was* putting out clouds of pollen, it didn't have any effect on her. Even when—

Suddenly, without warning, it all made sense. Her dreams, she realized, had been trying to talk to her all night, but she hadn't been listening.

Until now.

They had been telling her about both kinds of plants spraying their pollen at her at the same time! It *was* Culpepper's plant that was killing the Trilobur! But it did it *only* if both plants were pollinating! If Trilobur was ready to receive pollen, but got it from Culpepper's plants instead of another Trilobur...

That had to be it. When she and Albert had visited the Mollusk Town patch, Culpepper's plant was pollinating, and the Trilobur were about to. Twelve hours later, after they'd begun pollinating, the Trilobur were dead.

"Albert!" Leaping to her feet, she raced the fifteen or twenty feet to where he still slept. "Albert!" She grabbed his shoulder and shook him awake.

Albert's eyes popped open as he jerked to a sitting position. "Don't tell me it's another fire!"

Olivia shook her head vehemently. "It's not another fire! I know what's causing the blight!"

A shiver of nervousness rippled over Olivia as the Dimorphodon flapped away to the south. The message it was carrying invited Esther to meet them at Gundagai. They were going to test Olivia's theory about the blight.

Actually, Gundagai had been Albert's idea. He'd

remembered that the plants at that patch, both Culpepper's and the Trilobur, had only been about ten days away from pollinating when they'd seen them. Gundagai was the first town they'd visited, a little more than a week before. So if Olivia was right, the blight would strike the Gundagai patch in a matter of days, when Culpepper's plants and the Trilobur entered their pollination phases.

"Do you think Esther will actually come?" Olivia asked nervously.

Albert shrugged. "I can't imagine anything more important to her right now than finding out what causes the blight."

"But will she *believe* us?" Olivia asked. "I mean, we were only sent out to—to take notes. Scientists were supposed to be the ones to figure out how the blight worked."

Albert grinned. "So you saved them some time. I think your theory makes a lot of sense, and so will Esther. Now are you going to stand around worrying or are we going to head for Gundagai?"

Olivia tried to swallow away her nervousness. "Gundagai," she said, turning to climb onto Hightop.

Another shiver rippled over her as Thunderfoot led the way onto the trail. It was going to be a long trip.

The return trip promised to be much easier than the original journey. For one thing, Hightop and Thunderfoot, whose foot seemed fully recovered, were now thoroughly familiar with the roads and trails. More importantly, they didn't have to stop and inspect every patch of Trilobur along the way. It began to look as if they'd reach Gundagai in no more than twenty-four hours. That would be a full day before the blight would—*if she were right*—strike.

They were also catching up with Culpepper, they realized after half a dozen villages. At each village they passed through, they asked if the botanist been through there yet, and of course he had. At each village, he had demanded to be shown any Trilobur patch near the village. He'd looked at it, made some harrumphing noises, taken a few notes, and asked lots of questions that no one could answer. Then he'd taken even more notes. Sometimes he'd spent half a day nosing around before going on his way, leaving a puzzled and often annoyed village behind.

Until Narandra.

At Narandra, Olivia didn't have to ask about Culpepper. The villagers came swarming out to hail them down as soon as they heard—or felt—Thunderfoot's approach. Gunnarson, the tall blond man who had shown them to the village Trilobur patch before, was frowning as he approached.

"Do you know of a strange dolphinback who calls himself Culpepper?" Gunnarson asked. "Does he work with you?"

Olivia couldn't help but grin at the description.

Albert nodded. "He's involved with it, yes. Why do you ask?"

"He showed up early this morning. He claimed he was investigating the blight, but when we tried to talk to him—" Gunnarson shook his head worriedly. "I fear he's gone mad! Rather than speak with us, he fled into the jungle."

For a moment, Olivia almost laughed, thinking Gunnarson must be joking. Culpepper? Fleeing into the jungle? But then she saw the look of utter seriousness not only on Gunnarson's face but on the faces of the other villagers.

At the same time, she realized that this could be big trouble. If Culpepper's plants really *were* the cause of the blight, they would have to be gotten rid of, as quickly as possible. Which meant they had to be found. All of them.

And Culpepper was probably the only person on Dinotopia who knew where they all were.

CHAPTER 12

Olivia frowned. "Why would he run away?"

"I don't understand either," Albert said. "Are you sure he didn't just go on toward Waterfall City?"

Gunnarson shook his head. "Positive."

As Gunnarson continued, it became clear what had happened. Culpepper had done the same thing at Narandra that he had done at every other village. Only one thing had been different at Narandra. When he'd mentioned how long he'd been in Dinotopia, someone had come up with the same idea Olivia had. The blight started a year or two after he arrived; therefore, maybe he was responsible.

At that point, everyone had wanted to ask him questions. No one meant him any harm, of course, but Culpepper, already nervous, didn't see it that way. And then someone riding a gentle but very lethal-looking Styracosaurus had approached him. Culpepper took one look at its naturally solemn face and the half-dozen sharp horns that stuck out like curved spears from its rock-hard neck frill.

And he bolted.

"He was like that Lee Crabb fella," Gunnarson said. "He was through here a few years ago, trying to find someone who'd help him 'escape.' And he just plain didn't believe *anything* anyone said to him, human or saurian. Neither would Culpepper."

Olivia nodded. She'd heard of Crabb, too. Hightop had even met him once, though he rarely talked about it. "A most unpleasant individual" was about all the Plateosaurus would say. Crabb had been on Dinotopia several years longer than Culpepper. Like Culpepper, he was still trying to find a way off the island. Worse, he had some crazy idea that all the humans were being held prisoner on the island by the dinosaurs. "Scalies," he called them.

"Anyway," Gunnarson finished, "we just wanted to know if he really *was* working with you or any of the Partners. And if you wanted us to try to bring him back."

"Bring him back?" Albert said. "You mean you know where he is?"

Gunnarson nodded. "We followed him. If you'd like to see—"

"Where is he?" Albert asked.

"Holed up in a Refuge four or five miles that way," Gunnarson said, gesturing to the southeast, "just this side of the river. We can take you to him."

One of the Polongo tributaries, Olivia thought. She and Albert were familiar with the area. They had passed through it on their way both to and from the spot checks. If they went there and were able to talk Culpepper into coming out, they'd be able to head cross-country, almost directly south, picking up the trail again halfway to Gundagai. They wouldn't lose *that* much time. Still, for all she knew, just a few minutes might be enough to make them too late.

"I'll go," Albert suddenly said. "Olivia, you go on to Gundagai. After all, it's your prediction we're going there to check. You deserve to be there."

Olivia protested, but only a little. Mostly, she felt relieved. She didn't really want any more to do with Culpepper than absolutely necessary. And she really did want to get to Gundagai's Trilobur patch and see if she'd been right about the blight hitting there.

And she *really* wanted to be there to tell Esther all about it in person!

As Thunderfoot carried them through the jungle toward Culpepper's Refuge, Gunnarson finished telling Albert about the botanist's situation.

"The Refuge is only a hundred feet or so short of the river," he said. "And once he was in there, we couldn't go in after him. You know how Refuges are stocked."

Albert nodded. Far back in each narrow-mouthed cave, beyond the reach of any meat-eater that might wandered across from Rainy Basin, were piles of rocks and heavy sticks. If a meat-eater tried to poke its nose inside, a sharp whack with a stick or a thrown rock would discourage it. Eventually, according to the theory, the intruder would get tired of being whacked on the nose and go look for a less painful meal.

Albert shook his head. But the sticks and stones could be even more effective against human pursuers...

The Refuge was one of the natural caves that abounded in the area. Trees and underbrush made the entrance so nearly invisible that Albert was surprised Culpepper had found it. Patches of the river were visible through the trees and ferns and vines beyond it.

The three villagers Gunnarson had left to watch Culpepper were peering through a particularly thick batch of undergrowth between a pair of massive ginkgo trees. Gunnarson slid quickly from Thunderfoot's back and joined them.

"He's stuck his head out a couple of times," one of them said, "but he always goes back inside. I don't think he's seen us."

Thunderfoot eyed the Refuge entrance suspiciously. "I hope you're not thinking of asking *me* to stick my head in there," he said over his shoulder to Albert.

Albert looked down at the Chasmosaurus in mild surprise. Normally he would never have expected a comment like that from Thunderfoot. Or a comment of any kind, for that matter. Albert smiled. It was probably Hightop's influence. Like the foot-stomping to announce their arrival at villages, which had probably been copied from Grundle and Hoover, the Triceratops who had accompanied them out of Waterfall City.

"Don't worry," Albert said. "I'll go talk to him. And you walk as quietly as you can."

A few yards from the Refuge entrance, Albert climbed down.

Not a sound came from the Refuge. Culpepper had almost certainly heard them approach, even though Thunderfoot had done his best to tiptoe.

Albert went to stand a few feet from the opening, just to one side. Culpepper wouldn't be able to pitch a rock at him without showing himself.

"Mr. Culpepper," he called. "This is Albert. You remember Olivia and me, don't you? You met us at Collicos. We were investigating the blight, and you said—"

"How on earth did you find me?" Culpepper's whispered voice echoed out of the Refuge.

"The people you think you're hiding from showed me. Now why don't you just—"

"You mean they're out there? With you?"

"There are four of them about fifty yards back, watching. Thunderfoot and I are the only ones right here."

"Thunderfoot? Oh, you mean that creature you ride."

"At least I'm not the creature hiding in a cave," Thunderfoot remarked.

Probably Hightop's influence again, Albert thought as he waved a shushing hand at the Chasmosaurus. "Why *are* you hiding, Mr. Culpepper? No one wants to hurt you."

"You don't think so, eh? Did they tell you what they accused me of?"

"They didn't accuse you of anything. It's just that when they found out you came to Dinotopia a year or two before the blight started, they couldn't help but wonder if there wasn't a connection."

"They chased me just to ask questions? You may be naive enough to believe that, young man, but you didn't hear them! I was stranded on this wretched island a couple of years before this so-called blight started, so I was obviously the cause! And when I tried to leave, that horrid creature came charging at me. If I hadn't been quick, I would certainly have been stuck like a bug on a pin! On *several* pins!"

Albert sighed. "If you mean the Styracosaurus, he was—"

"I don't know what the creature is called. All I know is, it had very sharp horns sticking out in all directions, and it was coming right at me!"

"He was only coming closer so he and his rider could talk to you without having to shout. Like I'm having to shout now."

"I didn't ask you to shout. I just want to be left alone."

"Mr. Culpepper, I promise you'll be safe if you come out. No one's going to blame you for the blight."

"So you say." Culpepper's voice was filled with uncertainty.

"So we all say. For one thing, I think Olivia has figured out what *is* causing the blight."

Another silence from within the Refuge, and then Culpepper's head poked out. He was scowling skeptically as he looked at Albert.

"That *child* has determined the cause of the blight?"

"I think so," Albert said, though in truth he had few doubts. "We'll know for sure tomorrow. In Gundagai. That's where we were all headed. Esther's going to meet us there."

"And what is in Gundagai that will prove the child right? Or wrong?"

"There's a patch of Trilobur there. If she's right, it will be dead by tomorrow night."

Culpepper's scowl only deepened. "I find this very difficult to believe, young man. That child is *not* a trained botanist. How could she possibly—"

"If you want to find out, come with us!" Albert snapped, his patience finally giving way.

Still scowling, Culpepper stuck his head far

enough out to look nervously in the direction of the distant villagers. Finally, he came the rest of the way out. His jacket and knee breeches had a number of rips, and his boots were dirty and scuffed. Even his face was smudged. A small twig was caught in one of the straps of his backpack.

"Personally," Thunderfoot said in a dinosaur whisper, "I think we should have left him in the cave."

Albert stifled a laugh as he glanced sideways at the Chasmosaurus. This was *definitely* Hightop's influence.

CHAPTER 13

As planned, Albert and Culpepper headed through the jungle toward the Gundagai trail. Thunderfoot bulldozed his way in an almost straight line, and Albert soon began to wonder if they might not be making better time than they would have on the trail itself, which was anything but straight. They might even get to Gundagai before Olivia and Hightop.

Not that everything was going well.

It took Culpepper only a mile or so to forget about his recent fright and to become his old pompous self. Worse, he constantly repeated himself. Within an hour, he'd told Albert twice about his discovery of *Arctium culpepperus* during his travels in the Orient. He still couldn't believe that no one in Dinotopia had need of its remarkable stomach-soothing properties.

"They just won't admit it," he sniffed.

He even insisted on showing Albert the sturdy, belt-mounted pouches he carried the seeds in. The contraption was, of course, his own personal design.

Without it, he almost certainly would have lost the seeds when the ship went down.

He also explained again and again how those seeds would make his fortune once he returned to England. And he *would,* of course, return to England as soon as he found someone willing to build him "a proper boat." Such people would be much easier to find as soon as he uncovered the *true* solution to the blight and everyone realized what they owed him.

Albert prided himself on his self-control, but Culpepper finally got under even his skin, especially when he went on and on about his and Olivia's "lack of any *scientific* botanical knowledge."

"If you must know," Albert blurted out, cutting Culpepper off in mid-boast, "those people in Narandra were right. The blight *is* your fault!"

Culpepper blinked at the sudden outburst, then gave Albert a smile that was just short of a pat on the head.

"Impossible," he said smugly. "According to your own history, this blight has struck your plants several times in the past. That could hardly be my fault. The blight must therefore be caused by something which has been here for millennia. It simply lies dormant most of the time and flares up every few centuries. It is a common pattern all over the world. As anyone with even a basic understanding of science would know."

"Or it was brought here by outsiders each of those other times, too!"

Culpepper's smile grew even more patronizing. "And what could I or anyone else have possibly brought that would have such an effect?"

"Your plant! Your *Arctium culpepperus!*"

Culpepper's smile froze for a second. Then he laughed. "Absurd! Don't you even remember what you found at Collicos barely a week past? Whatever killed the Trilobur also killed my *Arctium culpepperus.*"

"We haven't figured that part out yet," Albert admitted. "But we will!"

"I'm sure you will. Perhaps you will also figure out why the two plants are growing quite well side by side any number of places. I have seen several such patches, even if you have managed to miss them."

"We didn't miss them! And Olivia already *has* figured out that part. They get along fine as long as they aren't both pollinating. When a Trilobur plant should be getting pollen from another Trilobur plant but instead it gets some from one of your plants, it can't handle it. And it dies!"

"Even more absurd!" Culpepper said heatedly. "Plants only accept pollen from other plants of their own kind! How else do you think it could ever work? In a single field there are often hundreds of different kinds of plants. Each puts out its own kind of pollen and accepts only that same kind from other plants. The air is filled with pollen of all kinds, but the plants simply *ignore* all pollen but their own brand."

"But what if it *can't* ignore some of it?" Albert demanded. "Just the way Olivia's eyes and nose can't ignore the pollen your plant puts out. Her eyes start itching and she starts sneezing whenever she gets near that plant—*if* it's putting out pollen."

"That's totally different!" the botanist exploded. "People aren't plants! That child is simply a human being who is *allergic* to a plant! Plants are not allergic to other plants!"

"How do *you* know?"

Culpepper shook his head in disbelief. "This is insane. There is no point in discussing this with—with an ignorant child!"

Albert forced himself to take a breath before replying. "We'll see who's ignorant tomorrow when that patch of Trilobur in Gundagai dies."

The remaining hour of daylight was spent in silence, except for the usual jungle sounds and the whispering rush of the nearby Polongo tributary. In his mind, however, Albert loudly scolded himself again and again for his outburst. For one thing, he really didn't like losing his temper. It invariably made matters worse. For another, what if Olivia was wrong? Just being wrong would be bad enough. But being wrong *and* being gloated over by someone like Culpepper would be truly awful.

But there wasn't anything he could do about it now. He just had to hope that Olivia was right. And that one of them could figure out the rest of the puzzle—why Culpepper's plant died along with the Trilobur.

They were still a couple of miles from the Gundagai trail when darkness forced them to stop for the night. Culpepper immediately spotted the entrance to another Refuge and announced that he wanted to stay there.

If he could get in.

Like the Refuge he had hidden in, it was in the side of a hill. Here, however, the entrance was almost completely blocked by a boulder. Several other rocks were scattered around the area, while a few remained at the top of the hill.

Albert wondered if the earthquake a couple years before had done this. It had temporarily blocked the Polongo far to the north, drying it up entirely for weeks. The quake had been felt all over this side of Dinotopia, so it certainly could have been responsible.

Culpepper struggled to push the rock back, but with no success. Even with Albert's help, he couldn't budge it. Finally, Thunderfoot relented and nudged it to one side. Even so, it remained perched precariously, looking as if a stiff breeze would send it tumbling back across the entrance.

Culpepper, however, was satisfied, and Albert, who had no intention of spending the night inside a place like that with the botanist, didn't care. He even grinned briefly as he imagined the boulder slipping back during the night.

When Albert was awakened at dawn by the sound of splashing water, however, he was suddenly glad the Refuge was there. Wading across the river less than fifty yards away was a meat-eater—a *big* meat-eater. An Allosaurus. Almost as big as a tyrannosaur, it had much longer front limbs with huge claws on each of its three fingers.

"Thunderfoot!" Albert hissed loudly, but there was no answer.

Looking around in the dim light from the reddening sky across the river, he couldn't see the Chasmosaurus anywhere.

Where *was* he, anyway? Munching on a particularly tasty leaf somewhere, most likely, but that wasn't any help right now. The Chasmosaurus could probably outrun the creature and carry them both to safety—if he were here to do so.

Lurching to his feet, Albert grabbed his backpack and raced toward the Refuge a dozen yards away. "Culpepper!" he called at the entrance. "We better get moving, and fast."

Culpepper, hair tangled and clothes even more wrinkled, stuck his head out of the entrance a few seconds later. "What—" he began, but then he heard the splashing and saw the Allosaurus, now almost completely out of the water.

And looking in their direction.

A moment later, Thunderfoot ambled out of the woods not far from the river bank. Even at a hundred yards, Albert could see a huge fern protruding from his mouth, bobbing up and down as he munched on it. But when he saw the Allosaurus, Thunderfoot abandoned his snack and started toward Albert at an earthshaking run.

Unfortunately, all he managed to do was attract the attention of the meat-eater, which was by now directly between the Chasmosaurus and the Refuge.

The Chasmosaurus stopped. He wasn't nearly as big as the Allosaurus, and he lacked the latter's deadly-looking claws and truly deadly teeth. He also lacked the other creature's belligerent temperament.

"Get inside the Refuge!" he honked loudly, a dinosaur version of a shout. "You'll be safe there until I can get help!"

"Be careful!" Albert shouted. "We'll be all right!"

The Chasmosaurus turned and thudded away through the jungle. The Allosaurus watched for a few seconds, then turned its attention to Albert.

"Come inside, young man!" Culpepper hissed urgently.

Albert stood watching as the creature headed straight toward them, not at a run but at a deliberate walk. Despite stories about such creatures, he wasn't sure they were as dangerous as they were made out to be.

As it drew closer, though, and the teeth grew ever

larger and sharper, Albert retreated to the Refuge entrance. He could hear Culpepper's heavy breathing in the darkness behind him.

Then the creature bolted forward. Startled at the sudden move, Albert lurched backward, banging his arm on the side of the entrance. Then he was inside, and the creature's snout was poking at the entrance.

Turning, Albert scrambled back to where Culpepper crouched. Grabbing up one of the sticks piled along one wall, he turned to the opening again. A moment later, a fist-sized rock came hurtling past his shoulder, hitting the creature's snout dead center.

For a moment, the Allosaurus did nothing. *Probably more startled than hurt,* Albert thought. Then it spread its huge jaws wide and let out a deafening bellow.

Albert grimaced, not so much at the noise but at the way the cave filled up instantly with the creature's bad breath. Meat-eaters were like that, he'd heard, but this was the first time he'd been close enough to find out for himself.

Another rock sailed past, larger this time, then another. With another smelly bellow, the Allosaurus pulled its head back from the opening.

And so they waited. After a few minutes, Culpepper, holding one of the heavier sticks, inched his way past Albert and peered cautiously out the entrance. Even more cautiously, he eased himself outside, darting nervous looks in all directions.

One slow step at a time, he made his way far enough from the entrance to see around the rock that had blocked it. As he leaned forward, there was a splashing sound from the river.

Culpepper jerked back, but then he gathered up his nerve and peeked around the edge of the rock toward the river. The splashing was still going on.

For a moment, the botanist seemed to slump in relief, his breath going out in a whoosh. But then he stiffened and ducked back behind the rock.

Flattening himself against the rock just outside the entrance, he looked toward Albert.

"Stay inside!" he said. "That splashing—it's another one coming across!"

Albert grimaced. "I hope Thunderfoot gets enough help," he muttered. Resignedly, he backed further into the Refuge.

Culpepper, instead of immediately following, eased cautiously forward once again to peek around the rock. Holding up a hand for Albert to stay back, he took another step forward.

And another.

Then he was easing himself around the rock once again. As he moved out of Albert's line of sight, he was still gesturing for him to stay back.

Albert frowned puzzledly. What was Culpepper up to? For someone who'd been frightened into hiding by a few villagers, he was suddenly being awfully brave.

Slowly, still clutching the large stick, Albert started forward. What was going on?

He was still six or seven feet from the entrance when there was a grunting sound from outside.

The rock shuddered and began to move.

For an instant, Albert couldn't bring himself to believe what was happening. For an instant, he stood frozen, and then it was too late.

As he lunged forward, dropping the stick, the huge rock tumbled from its precarious perch and thudded back into the depression it had occupied before.

The entrance was once again sealed.

CHAPTER 14

"Culpepper!" Albert shouted, pounding his hands against the rock. *"What happened?"*

But he was afraid he already knew.

For several seconds there was only silence. The distant splashing had faded before the rock had sealed the entrance.

Finally there was the faint sound of footsteps crossing in front of the rock. An inch-wide sliver of Culpepper's face appeared in the crevice along the right side of the rock.

"I'm sorry, young man, but I saw my chance and I had to take it." The botanist's voice was strained. "The creature has gone back across the river. That was the splashing you heard, not a second one coming to this side. I'm sure you'll be perfectly safe in there until your saurian friend returns to release you."

Albert blinked in the near-darkness of the cave. "But why?"

"I truly am sorry," Culpepper repeated, at least *sounding* sincere. "I mean you no harm. I only need to have a chance to speak with Esther before you and that other child bombard her with your wild theories. She might even believe them, since she probably has little more scientific knowledge than the two of you."

"But just because you get to her first, you think she'll believe you?"

"I can only hope." The sliver of face disappeared, and all Albert could hear were the botanist's retreating footsteps.

"You think she'll still believe you when she finds out what you did to me?" Albert shouted after Culpepper. "And Olivia's probably already *in* Gundagai!"

Culpepper's footsteps seemed to falter, but only for a moment.

Then they continued and soon were gone.

Albert shouted until he was out of breath, but there was no response. Culpepper had actually left!

At first Albert angrily paced back and forth in the narrow cave. But he soon calmed down enough to realize he wasn't accomplishing anything, just banging his elbows on the cave walls now and then.

Then he tried to work on the unanswered parts of the Trilobur puzzle. But he couldn't concentrate. All he could think about was getting out of the Refuge and telling Esther what the botanist had done. He was, he thought glumly, starting to act like Olivia, letting his emotions get the better of him.

The sun was well up into the sky when he heard—

or felt—the unmistakable thudding of his saurian partner's approach. Lurching to the entrance, he peered through the crevice but could see nothing.

"Thunderfoot!" he shouted as the thudding grew louder and closer. It even rattled the pile of sticks at the back of the Refuge.

Suddenly, the thudding stopped and something blocked the crevice entirely. A moment later, the boulder began to rock, then it rolled ponderously to one side, this time all the way out of the entrance so there was no chance it would roll back.

Thunderfoot lowered his head and peered inside puzzledly.

"What in the world happened?" he asked. "And where is everyone else?"

"I'll tell you in a minute," Albert said as hurried out of the Refuge. "But right now we have to get to Gundagai and—"

He broke off abruptly as he saw Hightop a few yards away. Olivia was perched on his back, looking confused. A pair of large Triceratops stood on either side.

"What are *you* doing here?" Albert asked, frowning. "I thought you were on your way—"

He broke off again, shaking his head. "Never mind. Explanations later. Right now we have to get to Gundagai!" He looked at the Triceratops. "The meat-eater went back across the river," he said. "But thank you for coming to help."

"You're welcome," one of the Triceratops honked, looking relieved at not having to face a dangerous meat-eater after all.

Albert was already scrambling onto Thunderfoot's back. "Let's go," he said urgently, wondering just how far Culpepper had gotten.

Once they were under way, Albert called back to Olivia and Hightop a few yards behind the trail-breaking Chasmosaurus. "You should be in Gundagai by now. Why are you here?"

"Well, I'm glad to see you, too!" Olivia called back. "We were just getting going this morning when I heard Thunderfoot thumping through the jungle. And he had this story about you being trapped by a meat-eater. I guess I figured leaving you to go after Culpepper on your own was bad enough."

She frowned. "Besides, I was worried about you. Anyway, it won't make any difference if I'm a little late at Gundagai. The Trilobur will get hit by the blight whether I'm there or not. The important thing is, Esther will be there to see it."

Albert shook his head. "That might've been true yesterday, but today's a different matter."

Grimly, he recounted everything that had happened with Culpepper.

"Even for a dolphinback," Hightop said indignantly when Albert had finished, "that is shockingly unacceptable behavior."

"But what does he think he'll be able to get Esther to do?" Olivia asked with a puzzled look.

"I'm not sure," Albert admitted. "He just wants the first shot at her, so he can convince her to believe him and not us. And he *is* a scientist—from the outside world, after all. Maybe she will believe him, no matter what he's done."

Olivia frowned, but she didn't disagree.

Thunderfoot quickly broke through to the Gundagai trail, but they still didn't make it to the village in time. They was still half a mile up the trail when Olivia saw a sky galley pulling up the last few feet of its rope ladder. Its air paddles were already spinning at full speed.

She couldn't see who was on it, but it had to be Esther. It only made sense that she would've come to Gundagai by sky galley rather than slog through the jungle.

By the time the group reached the village, the sky galley was little more than a distant dot heading back to Waterfall City.

They went directly to the Trilobur patch. Barlow, the young man who had proudly shown them to the patch before, was there along with several others. All were taking meticulous notes, some drawing detailed maps.

And the dozen or so Trilobur plants that had been close to pollinating last time were now shriveled and dead. All but one of Culpepper's plants still looked perfectly healthy, as did several Trilobur plants in other stages of development.

Olivia sighed with relief. She'd been right. And thanks to the villagers, Esther and the Partners would have a very good record of was going to happen next, as Culpepper's plants and the rest of the Trilobur would start to die.

She was less relieved when Barlow and the others told her and Albert what had happened. Culpepper had managed to hitch a ride with a friendly stegosaur and arrived while Esther was examining the blighted Trilobur. He hadn't stopped talking the whole time.

Whatever he'd said, it must have impressed her. She invited him to go with her in the sky galley back to Waterfall City for a meeting in Round Table Hall.

With a sinking feeling, Olivia climbed back onto Hightop. Albert took the Dimorphodon from its basket on Thunderfoot's back and handed it up to her.

"Find Esther," she told it. "She's on that sky galley on the way to Waterfall City. Maybe you can catch it." She and Albert then composed a brief message explaining as much about Culpepper and the blight as they thought the creature could remember.

Finally, it flapped into the sky in the same direction the sky galley had taken a couple hours earlier. Before it was out of sight, Olivia and Albert had started for Waterfall City. Rather than follow the winding trail they had followed on the way up, Thunderfoot commenced breaking a new trail, just as he had done earlier in the day. It might be more difficult, but it would almost certainly be faster.

As they went crashing through occasional clearings, Olivia and Albert scanned them on the fly. At most, they noted if there was Trilobur there and if it looked healthy. Also, they looked to see if there were any of Culpepper's plants nearby. They didn't need to inspect them closely to see if they were pollinating. Olivia's nose and eyes told her that.

They both knew from the start that, no matter how they rushed, Waterfall City was at least a day away. If they had started at dawn, they *might* have reached Sweetwater Lake by nightfall, but it was already early afternoon.

For a time, she hoped that the sky would remain clear and they could continue by moonlight, but that hope was short-lived. Long before sunset, clouds rolled in from the southwest, growing ever thicker as evening approached. At that point she began to hope that as long as the clouds would be blocking the moonlight they would at least bring some rain. She hadn't seen any fires since the one at Mollusk Town, but more than once she had caught a whiff of distant smoke.

And Waldemar, she knew, was still out there. Almost certainly there were several others just like him. They were still convinced that fire was the only way to stop the blight, and they were constantly searching it out. Even as careful as Waldemar had been, one of his fires had gotten away from him and Delphinia. If it hadn't been for the dozens of villagers and Thunderfoot and Hightop, it could have been a major disaster.

Olivia doubted that all the others were as cautious as Waldemar. All it took was one person to start a fire that would take hundreds to put out.

If it could be put out at all.

Once again she looked at the gathering clouds and hoped that they would indeed bring rain.

But they didn't, at least not anywhere near where they were. All they brought was the promise of an early end to the day's travel.

And then, just as the light was beginning to fade, Thunderfoot crashed through a particularly dense clump of undergrowth and emerged into another clearing. Hightop, with Olivia clinging to his back, was only seconds behind.

As she had a dozen times before, she sent her eyes darting about the clearing, searching for Trilobur and Culpepper's plants. By now, she was doing it automatically, expecting nothing new.

But this time she was wrong. This time, hundreds of Trilobur plants flashed into view, one of the biggest patches she had ever seen. Several of the Trilobur plants were dead of the blight, and Culpepper's plants were everywhere.

And this time, a pattern virtually leaped out at her.

"Stop!" she shouted at the top of her lungs. *"Stop!"*

CHAPTER 15

Hightop did his best to stop, but he had crossed the clearing and was into the underbrush on the far side before he could bring his tonnage to a complete halt. Ahead of them, Thunderfoot skidded to an even more jolting stop, sending Albert pitching against his huge, bony crest.

"I *thought* we were in a hurry," Hightop said, twisting his head around to look at Olivia.

"So did I," Albert grumbled. Bouncing off Thunderfoot's crest had obviously shaken him. "I assume you saw something important?"

Olivia nodded, her heart racing. Suddenly, she was afraid to go back and look more closely at the patch. Out of the corner of her eye, the pattern had been obvious. What if it had been her imagination?

With a gulping swallow, she jumped down and raced back to the clearing.

She almost went limp with relief.

The pattern really was there. Not as clean and clear

as it had looked out of the corner of her eye, but still there.

"Well?" Albert had climbed down and come to stand just behind her.

She blinked. Was it possible he didn't see it?

"There," she said, pointing at the center of the patch. "It's the blight, just like at Gundagai. But look at the rest of the Trilobur. And all those plants of Culpepper's."

"A lot of them are dying, too," he said. "But we already knew the blight killed them, just more slowly."

Olivia shook her head. He *didn't* see the pattern. Although it wasn't nearly as obvious down here as it had been from several feet up on Hightop's back.

"Come on," she said, leading the way into the heart of the patch. "Here, you can see the ones the blight killed." She pointed at nearly a dozen Trilobur plants grouped close together, dead and shriveled almost out of existence.

Albert nodded. "And there are several of Culpepper's plants, some dead, some dying," he said, looking around. Suddenly, he frowned.

"You see it?" Olivia asked.

"I *think* so," he said. He looked at her questioningly. "A series of concentric rings?"

She nodded emphatically. It was like a target, except the rings were jagged and incomplete and they overlapped wildly.

But they *were* rings.

The plants the blight had struck down first were in the very center, in the bull's-eye. In the innermost ring, the plants were almost as long-dead as the blighted ones. In the next ring out, they were just starting to shrivel. In the next ring, they were still clinging to life. In the next, they were just beginning to show the signs, just beginning to wilt. And beyond that, there were only healthy plants, not yet stricken. Both Trilobur and Culpepper's.

Death was spreading outward from the blighted plants. Spreading slowly.

Suddenly, like the pattern itself, the *reason* for the pattern came to her.

"It's spreading through the ground," she said. "It has to be!"

A poison of some kind was oozing out of the roots of the blighted Trilobur. Roots fat with the substances that, in Trilobite Tea, gave humans long life and health. But those same substances, when the plant was struck by the blight, were transformed into a poison that would eventually kill its attacker, *Arctium culpepperus*.

Self-defense.

But because the Trilobur was so similar to Culpepper's plant—so similar it could be fooled into taking in the other plant's pollen—the poison killed it, too.

Unable to contain herself, Olivia rattled off her theory to Albert and the two saurians. She was half expecting Albert to point out some mistake she had made, some blindingly obvious reason why it was impossible.

Instead, he nodded vigorously.. "That would explain why the blighted patches had to be burned before Trilobur would grow there again." He sounded almost as elated as Olivia felt. "Remember what Waldemar said about fire 'cleansing' the soil? He was right. Fire *burns* the poisons out of the ground! It all makes sense!" He laughed. "This should convince even Culpepper!"

But for anyone to be convinced of anything, they had to get to Waterfall City. And twilight was rapidly turning into night.

They managed only a few hundred yards more before total darkness closed in and they were forced to stop.

Even with the pitch blackness of the night, though, Olivia was too keyed up to go to sleep quickly or easily. Round Table Hall was so vivid in her mind she could almost see it. And her own words, her explanation of how the blight worked and how it could be stopped played themselves over and over in her imagination. She couldn't shut it down no matter how hard she tried.

But finally—she had no idea when—sleep came.

Hightop's urgent honks of "Fire!" awakened Olivia, setting her heart pounding.

For a moment she thought she was dreaming

again, reliving the fire at Mollusk Town, but then Albert was yanking her to her feet. The wind was hot and blustery. Above the treetops, smoke and sparks and flaming leaves whipped through the air.

"Someone must've set fire to that patch we saw tonight!" Albert shouted as he turned and raced to Thunderfoot. "We've got to get out of here!"

Without realizing quite how she did it, Olivia found herself on Hightop's back, struggling to get into her backpack straps while the Plateosaurus thudded through the trees and underbrush behind Thunderfoot.

Suddenly, flames erupted from the top of a tree almost directly in their path. Burning debris carried forward by the wind had swooped down, igniting the tinder-dry leaves of the tree's crown.

Almost immediately, the flames leaped to the top of a second tree and were threatening a third. Thunderfoot and Hightop veered to the left and managed to get past before the flames spread downward through the branches.

"The forest ends just ahead," Albert called back to her. "We should be all right once we get there."

Olivia didn't say anything, merely hung on as Hightop moved faster than she'd ever seen him move before. His head was down, avoiding the lower branches as he ran. Olivia had to duck her own head more than once. Albert also stayed low, hiding behind the Chasmosaurus's huge, shieldlike crest.

Then, suddenly, the forest ended and they burst out onto an uneven, grassy plain.

And they realized that though they were out of the forest they were far from being out of the woods. Not all of the wind-blown fragments of flame had fallen into the treetops. Many had whisked beyond the forest and onto the field. There they had plummeted down into grass that was even drier than the forest treetops.

A hundred yards to their right at least a dozen patches of flame had already flared up and were quickly merging into a single wall of fire. To the left, it was the same. New flames were springing up in the blink of an eye.

They were, all four of them realized, in the center of a corridor walled with fire. And it was growing longer with every passing second as the flames raced ahead of the wind through the tinder-dry grass. Worse, it was growing narrower, though not as rapidly. The wind wasn't driving either of the walls toward them, but it wasn't holding them back, either.

However, unless Hightop and Thunderfoot could run with the speed of a Velociraptor, there was no way they were going to outrace the flames and escape before the walls met.

"We have to go back!" Olivia shouted looking back at the wall of trees behind them. "The fire can't be *everywhere!*"

Without stopping his pell-mell flight, Hightop

stretched his serpentine neck up as far as it would go and looked back. After only a second, he lowered it. If anything, he increased his pace. "There is smoke almost everywhere," he honked, sounding out of breath for the first time Olivia could remember. "And where there isn't, there is fire."

But even as the Plateosaurus talked, a momentary gust of wind three or four hundred yards ahead—generated by the fire itself, she wondered?—narrowed the end of the corridor, then closed it altogether.

They were trapped.

CHAPTER 16

"Isn't there supposed to be a creek around here somewhere?" Olivia shouted at Albert.

"Beyond the fire," he shouted back, pointing toward the right wall of flame.

"Use your canteens," Hightop said. "Douse your blankets and wrap yourself in them and duck down as low as you can. If we run through the fire fast enough—"

"Don't be silly!" Olivia snapped. "No blanket's big enough for *you!* And even if we had one, there's not enough water in the canteens!"

"She's right," Albert shouted over the ever-louder crackle of the flames.

But what other choice did they have? Looking back, Olivia saw that the flames had already engulfed the part of the forest they had just left. At least the fire wasn't moving as fast as it had been. Had the wind slackened a little?

She shook her head. It wouldn't matter if the wind died out entirely. The damage had been done. They

126

were surrounded by flames, and in a few minutes the whole area would look just like the burned-out patches of Trilobur. Nothing but ashes.

Nothing but ashes!

Ashes don't burn!

"Stop right here!" she shouted at Hightop. "You, too, Thunderfoot! I've got an idea!"

The Plateosaurus looked back at her for a moment, then lurched to a stop, followed a moment later by Thunderfoot.

Olivia scrambled off Hightop's back, shrugged out of her backpack, and began digging frantically through it. After a few seconds, she came up with her tinderbox and flint. As dry as the grass was, she might not even need the tinder. But there was no taking chances.

Legs trembling, Olivia dropped to her knees in the grass and pulled out the almost hair-thin tinder and laid it on the ground.

"What are you doing?" Albert shouted.

"Get behind me!" she shouted back. "Upwind!"

And she began striking the flint and steel together.

Or trying to. On the first stroke, she hit her own fingers.

Heart pounding so hard she could feel the thumping against her tunic, she took a deep breath and tried again. And again. But the tiny sparks, almost invisible in the light from the approaching flames, vanished before they reached the tinder. Out of the corner of her eye, she could see Hightop urging the others to follow her instructions and get behind her.

Which wouldn't help if she couldn't get a decent spark!

Leaning closer, she brought her trembling hands down until they were almost touching the tinder.

And the tinder caught.

An instant later, the grass around it caught as well.

"Grab a handful of grass, like a torch!" she shouted at Albert. Without waiting to see what he did, she grabbed a handful herself, yanked it free, and held it to the flames.

"If we can burn off a large enough piece of ground right now, right here," she shouted as her makeshift torch caught, "there won't be anything left for the big fire to burn when *it* gets here!"

Comprehension dawned on Albert's face, and he grabbed a handful of the long grass himself. A moment later, he was hurrying to the left, dragging his torch along the top of the grass as Olivia did the same to the right. Hightop turned his back to the new flames and vigorously swished his long tail back and forth like a giant fan.

To Olivia's huge relief, the wind gusted up again, fanning the newly lit flames and driving them forward. But the same gust sent more sparks and flaming leaves sailing through the air from the forest line. One dropped to the ground well ahead of the main wall of flame.

Thunderfoot saw it first and instantly lumbered toward it, the ground shaking as he thudded through the grass. He was on it almost before the grass caught fire, his massive feet stomping it out before it could spread.

A second airborne spark was defeated by Albert, who tossed his torch down and snatched up his blanket. With all his canteen's water soaking it, the blanket was almost as effective as Thunderfoot's stomping. Olivia, armed now with her own blanket, caught a third.

By then the main wall of flame was bearing down on the point where the first spark had fallen, and they retreated hastily.

They didn't have far to retreat. The fires she and Albert had set still burned. They were not yet unburnable ashes, and Olivia wondered if her frantic actions had helped or hurt them.

Even as the thought came to her, the nearest flames began to turn to smoke as the last of the tinderlike grass was consumed. With her blanket, she flailed at the growing burned-out area, and Albert joined her a moment later.

Finally, there was room for the two saurians, though Olivia wondered if their unshod feet would need more Trilobur salve when it was all over. Even among the crumbling ashes, there were spots that still smoldered. She could feel the heat through the soles of her own heavy boots.

But there were no honking complaints. All four worked together in silence to expand the safe area as the whoosh and crackle of the main walls of flame grew ever louder, ever closer.

Five yards of smoldering ashes, then ten, then twenty, and the advancing flames reached the edge of the burned-out area.

And stopped.

Twenty yards to either side, beyond the blanket of ashes, the flames continued to advance, overtaking the flames Olivia and Albert had set.

They waited, saying nothing, feeling the heat beating at them from all sides until, finally, only ashes and wisps of smoke separated them from the forest. The dry grass had been entirely consumed. They were safe.

But in the forest, where trees and brush and ferns and a hundred other plants provided infinitely more fuel, the fire still raged. If they been trapped there, Olivia knew, they wouldn't have had a chance.

Finally, by mid-afternoon, the fire was out. Humans and saurians from miles around had seen the flames and come running. Everyone, including the woman who had started the fire, worked without a moment's break. Water was hauled. Strips of land were cleared. Other fires were set like the one Olivia had set, only with more time for planning and safeguards.

And the wind, blessedly, had shifted and then almost died out.

Then began the long process of making sure it didn't start up again. After a brief rest, people and saurians alike began roaming systematically across the fields of ash, dousing and stamping out any sparks that remained. That night, a pair of Skybaxes would take turns circling over the charred forest.

Olivia and Albert, both of them dirty and soot-stained and exhausted, didn't take time to rest. As soon as the way to Waterfall City was once again open, they were on their way. The fire had only made it more urgent that they reach Esther and Round Table Hall quickly.

By sundown they were still many miles from their goal. This time, however, they were in luck. The sky remained clear, and the moon, though no longer quite full, made travel possible, though not easy or fast.

To Olivia's surprise, a ferry was waiting at Sweet-water Lake when they finally arrived. She had expected they would have to wait, most likely until morning. But there it was, the same ferry that had taken them across before. Its plump, white-haired captain, with his neatly trimmed goatee and gold-braided uniform, greeted them as they approached.

"Esther and the Partners will be relieved to see that you're safe," he said. "We received word of a burning that got out of control. It was said to be somewhere along the route you were taking, and we were all concerned. I take it from your appearance that you were indeed involved."

Olivia grimaced. "A lot more than I wanted to be," she said. Albert just nodded.

As she spoke, the captain stepped up on his raised platform and looked off toward Mosasaur Harbor. Its lights were dimly visible through the mist from the falls. Picking up a large lantern, he adjusted it so that its light was directed in a single direction.

Then he held it aloft, high over his head, and pointed it toward the harbor for several seconds. Then he lowered and raised it again. Five times he repeated the action, holding himself as steady as he could as Hightop and Thunderfoot came on board.

In answer, a tiny light appeared at the dark mouth of the harbor. It shone for a few seconds, then vanished. Appeared and vanished again.

"What was *that* all about?" Olivia asked when he set the lantern down.

"Like I said, missy," the captain said, "people are interested in your safe return." This time, unlike the first time they'd met, there was no trace of humor or good-natured sarcasm in his voice.

With that, he shouted a signal to the plesiosaurs harnessed to the ferry, and they were on their way.

Because of the ferry captain's signals, Olivia half expected to find Esther and the Partners waiting for them when they reached the harbor. Instead, they were greeted by two young men in long red coats and two-pointed hats.

"Esther and the Partners have been informed of

your safe arrival," the taller one said. "She asks that tonight you rest and refresh yourself from your ordeal. In the morning, she will greet you herself at Round Table Hall."

"But we have important information—" Olivia protested.

"Esther and the Partners assumed that was the case," the shorter one said. "Nonetheless, she desires that you have patience. Nothing can be accomplished before morning except your rest and recuperation."

Moments later, the two saurians were directed to the massive Sauropod Dwelling. Olivia and Albert, despite their protests, were each plumped into one of the wheelbarrow-like human-powered taxis and delivered to the Haven. Olivia had to admit that she rather enjoyed the ride.

Once at the Haven, they were shown to rooms and given meals that apparently had been especially saved for them both.

Later, scrubbed and as relaxed as she had been in days, Olivia lay in bed and decided that Esther had been right. Whatever mischief Culpepper was up to, it wouldn't be any worse in the morning.

And she, after sleeping indoors for the first time in several days—in a sinfully soft bed, at that—*definitely* wouldn't be any worse.

This time, even the constant rumble of the falls thundering into Cloudbottom Gorge couldn't keep her awake.

CHAPTER 17

Morning found another of the red-coated young men at Olivia's door with another meal. He waited while she ate, then escorted her to the Haven's entrance. There Albert and another red-coat joined them.

Hightop and Thunderfoot were just entering the building housing Round Table Hall when Albert and Olivia arrived. Hurrying in after them, they were startled to see only Esther waiting for them outside the grand meeting room.

"What did Culpepper say?" Olivia asked as she rushed up to Esther. "He told me he was going to convince you that—"

"Now, now, my dear," Esther said, holding her hands up as if to fend off Olivia's flood of words. "Don't concern yourself with Professor Culpepper."

"But he said his plants *couldn't* be the cause of the blight, but they *are!*"

"She's right," Albert put in. "Not only that—"

"I know," Esther said. "I plan to send Dimorphodons out to as many villages as possible, to spread the word. The Partners—"

"But he said you'd *have* to listen to him, not Albert or me! He's a scientist, and we're just—"

"I told you, don't concern yourself with Professor Culpepper," Esther said with soft laugh. "I'm quite familiar with him, and I think I know when to believe him and when not."

"You know him?" Olivia and Albert chorused.

Esther nodded. "Quite well, as a matter of fact. He came to us the first year he was on our island. He seemed to think we were all complete ignoramuses since we didn't have all the latest discoveries in botanical science at our fingertips. And he insisted that our belief that Trilobur kept us young was nothing but superstition." She chuckled. "When I told him I was a hundred and seventy-five, he acted as if I were feeble-minded."

"He still doesn't believe it," Olivia said, while Albert nodded his agreement. "The only reason he wants to find a way to stop the blight is so people will be grateful enough to him to give him what he wants. Which is a boat to escape in."

"I know," Esther said, shaking her head sadly. "I thought he would get over his obsession to 'escape,' but he hasn't. In fact, that was one of the reasons we sent him around the island to survey the plant life. We thought that surely if he traveled all across the island, along the entire coastline, he'd realize it really *is* impossible to leave. And if he talked to enough people, he'd even begin to believe that Trilobur really does what we say it does."

"What about his survey?" Olivia asked. "He said he had scrolls full of observations. Are they worth anything?"

Esther smiled ruefully. "We may never know. He wrote everything in English and won't let the scrolls out of his sight, not even to be translated."

Olivia sighed. "He thinks they're going to make him famous when he gets back to England. And his plant is going to make him rich. They must have an awful lot of indigestion in England."

"I've heard they have a lot of it everywhere out there. Because of the way they live, some say."

Hightop gave a saurian snort of amusement. "If they're all like Professor Culpepper," he honked, "it's no wonder." The Plateosaurus lowered his head toward Esther. "I believe you know what Culpepper did to Albert! You did receive the message we sent, didn't you?"

Esther nodded but smiled faintly. "I don't think Culpepper is that bad, underneath it all."

The Plateosaurus drew back, arching his serpentine neck. "I must say, I'm surprised to hear you say that," he honked quietly. "Personally, I find his behavior utterly reprehensible."

"As do I," Esther said, "but one must make allowances for dolphinbacks. Admittedly, he is taking longer than most to adjust. However, he *is* genuinely sorry for what he did to Albert, trapping him in that Refuge. And when he heard about the burning, he was extremely upset."

"I should hope so!" Hightop said stiffly. "Because of him, we came within an egg tooth of being incinerated."

Olivia, however, suddenly grinned. "Did it give him more indigestion?" she asked.

"As a matter of fact, young lady, I believe it did," Esther said, smiling back.

Before she could say more, the massive door to the street opened again and a steady stream of Habitat Partners flowed through, heading for Round Table Hall. Several of them acknowledged Olivia and Albert with a nod or a smile. In their midst, however, was Culpepper. When the botanist saw the pair, he ducked his head and looked fixedly at the floor as he hurried by.

"Go on in," Esther said. "There are a few things I have to take care of before the meeting gets under way."

With that, she turned and hurried over to Bracken and Fiddlehead, the Forest Partners, just as they entered the Hall. Too late, Olivia realized she *still* hadn't told Esther about how the blighted Trilobur poisoned the ground all around it.

Grimacing, she joined the stream flowing into the Hall. Albert was just behind her. Once inside, they climbed onto their ladderlike chairs and looked around nervously. She'd never seen this many Partners gathered together—except in that one silly dream. Suddenly, she realized that besides Esther, she, Albert, Hightop, and Thunderfoot were the only non-Partners there.

Except for Culpepper, of course, who was shifting nervously in his seat, looking everywhere except at Olivia and Albert. Olivia wondered how his indigestion was doing.

Finally, Esther climbed into her seat.

"Gentlebeings," she began, "you all know why we are here today. A likely cause of the Trilobur blight has been discovered. We must decide, first, if we are confident enough in that discovery to take action. Second, we must decide precisely what action, if any, we are to take."

Everyone murmured or nodded their silent approval. Everyone but Culpepper, who looked grimly at Esther.

Before Esther could continue, Culpepper interrupted sharply. "I am indeed aware of your plans and this so-called discovery," he said. He looked quickly around the table, though still avoiding Olivia and Albert.

"Yes, Professor Culpepper?" Esther said. "I believe you have something you wish to say to us all."

"Indeed I do." Again he looked around the table. Again his eyes lowered momentarily as his gaze swept past Olivia and Albert. "You have all been told that the plant I brought to this island, *Arctium culpepperus,* is the cause of the blight. I assure you it is not. I am a trained botanist, a scientist, and I assure you that plants simply do not act this way."

"Then how do you explain the evidence?" Bracken asked. "At Gundagai, it was predicted that the blight would appear, and it did. Those Trilobur plants that were pollinating died when your plants entered their pollination phase. Are you saying this is mere coincidence?"

"Ah!" Culpepper said, suddenly smug. "You've left out one important fact: This so-called blight also killed my *Arctium culpepperus!* The only difference is my plants were not killed as quickly. But I personally saw three of my plants beginning to wilt the very day after the Trilobur plants died. And the same was true in the patch near Collicos. The blight struck there several weeks before, and not a single *Arctium culpepperus* survived. It may have taken two or three weeks for them to wilt and die, but every single one did. So how can they be the *cause* of the blight if they are also the victims?"

"I can explain it!" Olivia blurted out.

All eyes turned toward her, even Culpepper's. He looked more angry than guilty now, though.

"Please do," Esther said, looking directly at Olivia.

Gulping, she glanced at Albert, who nodded encouragingly.

And she explained.

She explained about the pattern she'd seen in the most recent burned patch. She explained her theory that the swollen roots of the blighted Trilobur produced a poison that seeped into the ground and killed not only Culpepper's plants but also any Trilobur nearby. And she explained why fire really did "cleanse" the soil.

"Preposterous!" Culpepper suddenly objected. "Even if this pattern *does* exist in one patch, what about all the others? It's just a coincidence!"

"It's *not* a coincidence!" Olivia said. "All the blighted patches we saw were like that!"

Culpepper snorted in disbelief. "And how could you possibly know that?"

"Because of Albert's notes," Olivia said. "We went back over them after we knew what we were looking for. The pattern was always there—we just didn't recognize it until now." She looked toward Albert.

The boy nodded. "She's right. Sometimes it was only half a dozen plants at different distances from the ones killed by the blight. You'd never see it unless they knew exactly what to look for. We didn't then, but now we do."

For a long moment, there was complete silence around the table. Even Culpepper said nothing.

Finally, Esther cleared her throat. "Well done, both of you," she said, then looked around at the Partners. "It seems we have our work cut out for us. Our first priority is to get word to Waldemar and the other firesetters, before yet another burning gets out of control. This information should be enough to get them uprooting Culpepper's plants rather than burning them when it's too late."

The Partners murmured their agreement. Then Esther turned toward Culpepper, who was staring stonily down at the table.

"Professor Culpepper," she said quietly. "Do you agree? Or do you have an alternative theory to account for the blight?"

For several seconds he remained silent and motionless except for a brief, pained grimace. His indigestion must really be kicking up, Olivia thought, beginning to almost feel sorry for him.

Finally, he looked up. "I am forced to admit that I cannot construct an alternative theory on the spur of the moment," he said stiffly. "Nor can I refute the one advanced by these...children. Except to say that it does not fit well with established scientific knowledge as I understand it."

"Nor, I imagine, do we," Hightop honked quietly. "And yet, here we are."

Culpepper grimaced and sighed. "Unfortunately true," he said. "In any event, there is nothing I can do to stop you from exterminating *Arctium culpepperus*, which I assume is your plan."

"In essence, yes," Esther said. "However, in light of your dependence on its medicinal properties, we will, of course, first harvest an ample supply of its roots for your use. And if you wish, you will be allowed to maintain an isolated patch of the plant."

Culpepper frowned skeptically. "I don't understand."

"It's quite simple, Professor Culpepper. Your continued good health—your digestive health—is dependent on a brew you make from your plant, just as our longevity is dependent on a brew we make from our Trilobur. It is not your fault that the plants are deadly to each other, so there is no reason for you to suffer."

"You would do this for me?" He looked from Esther to the Partners and back. "Even though you think the blight is my doing?"

"Of course," she said, and the Partners nodded. "You did not do it intentionally, so why would we not?"

Again he fell silent, then looked toward Olivia and Albert. "Even you?"

Olivia shrugged, realizing she really *was* feeling sorry for him. She glanced at Albert, who nodded and said, "As long as you promise not to seal me up in any more Refuges."

Culpepper winced, then sighed and looked back at Esther. "If it will help," he said, "I kept a complete record of the time and location of every planting."

"That would be most helpful, Professor Culpepper," Esther said. "And later, perhaps you would consent to having your entire journals translated. I imagine there is information there that could prove valuable in other ways."

"Of course," Culpepper said, after hesitating only slightly.

"However," Esther went on, looking around at the others. "There is still one other problem, perhaps the most immediate one. *Arctium culpepperus* has apparently spread far beyond the places where it was first planted. It will doubtless be difficult to find them all. Does anyone have any ideas?"

Olivia grimaced as she remembered her first eye-watering encounter with Culpepper's plant. But what other choice was there?

With a sigh, Olivia raised her hand.

CHAPTER 18

Olivia sneezed violently, then tightened her grip on the specially made Skybax saddle for two. Without the special handholds—and an experienced rider to guide the Skybax—she couldn't have stayed on for more than a few seconds. If the sneezes didn't throw her off, the twists and turns of treetop-level flying would have.

"Another one?" Dorian asked. One of the smallest and most experienced of the Skybax riders, he had worked diligently with his mount for more than a week to convince it to accept a second rider, a passenger.

"Another one," she snuffled, risking letting go of one handhold long enough to wipe at her eyes and nose.

"We'd better go down and pinpoint it," Dorian said.

Olivia grimaced and nodded. "I guess we'd better."

First, though, Dorian sent the Skybax spiraling upward two or three hundred yards until he spotted Hightop and Thunderfoot nearly a half mile away.

When he was certain the two saurians and Albert had seen him, he nudged the Skybax into a descending spiral. The maneuver would let them know where he was landing.

This time they were landing in an open meadow in Blackwood Flats, so it was easy. In some of the heavily wooded areas, they hadn't been able to find a clearing within half a mile of the offending plants.

Still, it took them nearly half an hour after they'd landed to zero in on Olivia's latest discovery. By that time, Albert and the two saurians were trailing close behind. There were only three plants, it turned out, and only one was spraying the air with its pollen.

Retreating out of pollen range, Olivia tried to re-lax as Albert uprooted the three and bagged them. Once the pollen settled, she and Dorian would have to make another series of airborne passes just to be sure there weren't others hidden nearby. Others would come to the site after that and make a thorough ground search of the entire area, looking for other plants that hadn't started pollinating yet. A few months later, the searchers would come again, just to be sure that seeds left behind by the original plants hadn't sprouted.

This time Olivia had also noticed a couple of Trilobur that weren't dying but, instead, were doing just the opposite. They were sprouting three or four times as many burs as a normal Trilobur, and they were doing it several times as fast. She had seen several plants like that since their search began. No one had noticed them before, because people had only been looking for blighted, dying plants. But soon she was seeing one of that kind for every five or six blighted ones. It almost certainly had something to do with the blight, but no one knew what. In hopes of finding out, Esther had ordered all such plants be transplanted to one of Professor Culpepper's glass-enclosed labs for him to study.

As for Culpepper, once he'd finally accepted that his plants really were the cause of the blight, he'd decided to try to find out how they caused it. He hadn't yet, nor had he learned what caused some Trilobur plants to grow extra-fast instead of die.

But he wasn't giving up. He was, in fact, trying just as hard now to learn the secrets of the blight—*all* the secrets—as he had tried before to escape from the island.

He was also using fewer and fewer of the roots Esther and the Partners had set aside for him. Apparently, his indigestion was gradually becoming less of a problem.

"Being a pompous know-it-all is hard on the digestion," Hightop had remarked when he'd heard of the improvement.

Finally, Dorian signaled to Olivia that it was safe to come back over. Albert had dug the plants up and sealed them in a bag. Now he was packing the bagged plants into a large wooden box on Thunderfoot's back.

While Albert sealed the lid on the nearly full box, Olivia took an eight-foot pennant from one of the huge saddle bags Hightop was carrying. With a solid thrust, she jabbed it into the ground where the plants had been. Later searchers would look for the colorful flag and start there.

Olivia was just climbing into the Skybax saddle next to Dorian when she noticed a sky galley approaching. Puzzled, she slid back to the ground and stood watching as the ship slowed and descended to only twenty or thirty yards.

It had barely stopped, its air paddles moving slowly to counteract a light breeze, when a rope ladder spilled over the railing. Albert grabbed the lower end and held it steady as someone started to descend.

"Esther!" Olivia gasped. What was *she* doing here?

Before Esther stepped off onto the ground, Hightop obligingly took hold of the ladder. With him as an anchor, the galley wouldn't have to vent gas in order to hold its position.

Esther glanced at the pennant a few yards away, then turned to Olivia, looking closely at her face. Olivia's eyes were still puffy.

"Is something wrong?" Olivia asked apprehensively.

Esther shook her head and smiled. "On the contrary, things are progressing quite well. We have found another like yourself who can 'sniff out' Culpepper's plants. That makes six altogether." .

"That's wonderful!" Albert said.

"Yes, it is," Olivia agreed. "But why did you come all the way out here to tell us?"

"Because I believe we have enough such 'sniffers' now to do the job without you."

Olivia blinked. For a moment, the prospect of never again sneezing, of never again having to wipe her itchy, watering eyes was overwhelmingly attractive. A few weeks ago, before the fires and all the rest, she would've accepted an offer like that without a second thought.

But now...

She shook her head. "Thanks, but I think I'll keep at it, if you don't mind."

Esther just smiled and nodded, but Albert looked at her with a puzzled frown.

"Olivia!" he said. "You've done *more* than your share. *Far* more."

"Maybe so," she admitted, unable to entirely suppress the warm glow his words and Esther's gave her. "But it's better if I keep going. The more 'sniffers' on the job, the sooner this whole thing will be over."

Which was very true. It wasn't, however, the only reason. There were others—reasons that had kept her from throwing up her hands in the face of each new misery-making attack.

For one thing, zooming around on a Skybax was pretty exciting, even with the sneezing.

For another, she knew that would-be apprentices stuck with jobs until they were done, especially the ones that weren't so easy. And that went for other things she didn't like so much either, like taking notes. If she really wanted to be an apprentice—and she really did—she was going to have to get used to it. Albert had promised to keep helping her.

And finally, it just plain felt good to be part of a team, particularly with Albert. When he'd heard her plan, he had insisted on being the one who followed along on the ground to do the digging and collecting.

But the team wasn't just her and Dorian and Albert and Hightop and Thunderfoot, though they might be the most important parts, at least to her. It included virtually all of Dinotopia. Even Culpepper. Which was another thing she couldn't have imagined herself thinking a few weeks ago.

"Come on, Dorian," she said, turning back to the waiting Skybax, "I should be good for at least one more sneezing fit before sundown."

REVISIT THE WORLD OF

DINOTOPIA

in these titles,
available wherever books are sold...

OR

You can send in this coupon (with check or money order)
and have the books mailed directly to you!

❑   *Windchaser* (0-679-86981-6) $3.99
     by Scott Ciencin

❑   *River Quest* (0-679-86982-4) $3.99
     by John Vornholt

❑   *Hatchling* (0-679-86984-0) $3.99
     by Midori Snyder

❑   *Lost City* (0-679-86983-2) $3.99
     by Scott Ciencin

❑   *Sabertooth Mountain* (0-679-88095-X) $3.99
     by John Vornholt

❑   *Thunder Falls* (0-679-88256-1) $3.99
     by Scott Ciencin

❑   *Firestorm* (0-679-88619-2) $3.99
     by Gene DeWeese

Subtotal .... $ _____

Shipping and handling .... $ 3.00

Sales tax (where applicable) .... $ _____

Total amount enclosed .... $ _____

Name _____

Address _____

City _____ State_____ Zip _____

Make your check or money order (no cash or C.O.D.s)
payable to Random House, Inc., and mail to:
Order Department, 400 Hahn Road, Westminster, MD 21157.

Prices and numbers subject to change without notice. Valid in U.S. only.
All orders subject to availability. Please allow 4 to 6 weeks for delivery.